ALSO BY SAYANTANI DASGUPTA

Secrets of the Sky

BOOK ONE

The Chaos Monster

Kiranmala and the Kingdom Beyond

BOOK ONE

The Serpent's Secret

BOOK TWO

Game of Stars

BOOK THREE

The Chaos Curse

The Fire Queen

BOOK ONE

Force of Fire

BOOK TWO

Crown of Flames

For Young Adults

Debating Darcy

Rosewood: A Midsummer Meet Cute

THE
POISON
WAVES

SECRETS OF THE SKY

BOOK TWO

THE POISON WAVES

SAYANTANI DASGUPTA

Illustrations by SANDARA TANG

SCHOLASTIC PRESS | *New York*

Library of Congress Cataloging-in-Publication Data available

ISBN 978-1-338-76675-2
10 9 8 7 6 5 4 3 2 1   23 24 25 26 27
Printed in Italy   183
First edition, October 2023
Book design by Abby Dening

For Baba

TABLE *of* CONTENTS

1

Mermaids Smell like Fish Scales

IF THERE WAS one thing that Kiya didn't like, it was mermaids.

"I hate mermaids!" she said for the zillionth time to her twin brother, Kinjal. "I can't believe Lola would choose such a babyish theme for her birthday party!"

"What d'ya want her to choose as her theme? The periodic table?" Kinjal gave a laughing snort at the cleverness of his own joke, making Kiya roll her eyes. Unlike her brother, she was a big fan of all science-y and scientific things.

Kinjal was, as usual, roughhousing with their dog, Thums-Up, who was chocolate colored and named after their mom's favorite childhood soda. Kinjal was hurling the dog's tennis ball around the living room in a way their parents would never let him do if they were home. But it was parent-teacher conference night, and for the first time in the twins' ten long years of life, Ma and Baba had agreed to leave them alone at home for the few hours they would be gone. Probably an unwise decision on their part. It wasn't that Kiya wanted, or needed, a babysitter. She was just sure that her brother was seconds away from breaking something. Also as usual.

"At least a periodic table of elements birthday party would be unique!" Kiya fixed one of her braids with a firm yank.

"Don't be boring. Now, a *warrior sloths*–themed party, *that* would be way awesome!" Kinjal enthused, naming the long-armed, slow-moving heroes of his favorite fantasy series.

Kiya's eyes narrowed behind her red-framed glasses. "Just because I'm not a walking chaos monster like you doesn't mean I'm boring!"

Chaos monsters were the mortal enemies of the warrior sloths, and also what she liked to call her brother. Because if anything, Kinjal was chaotic. And sometimes, in her opinion, also monstrous.

"Just because you're a perfect, never-make-a-mistake control freak doesn't mean I'm a chaos monster!" Kinjal said in between throws of the dog's tennis ball, which bounced off the walls, furniture, and floor.

"Who are you calling a control freak, you . . . you"— Kiya tried to think of a suitable insult—"*freak* freak?"

"Was that the best you could come up with?" Kinjal snorted. "Anyway, way to rub it in, Dr. Perfecto-Pants. I'm not even invited to Lola's mermaid birthday bash."

"I could ask if you could come." Kiya smartly caught the tennis ball before her brother could knock the giant, messy bag of Cheetos he was snacking on from the end table. Not to mention the lamp that also sat there. "To the party, I mean."

"No way." Kinjal jammed some more Cheetos into his already-orange-lipped mouth. Even his shaggy hair had some Cheeto dust in it, making him look like he'd gotten some kind of weird punk rock dye job. "Don't ask Lola to include me. I don't need a pity invite."

Thums-Up gave a low whine, as if she was agreeing, and Kinjal tossed her a Cheeto, which she caught midair with a loud, messy crunch.

Mermaid-birthday-party Lola was their next-door neighbor, who Kiya had made friends with a few weeks ago only to make her brother, Kinjal, jealous. And now, because of that one bad decision, Kiya was the proud owner of a sparkly, peacock-colored birthday party invitation with a red-haired, sparkly-tiara-wearing mermaid on the front. I mean, if there was anything Kiya hated more than mermaids, it was tiaras. Oh, and sparkles. Gah.

Kiya stared at the card like she was trying to set it on fire with a death glare. "It would be better if you were there," she said in a small voice.

Despite all the bad things about being her brother's twin, one of the good things was always having him right next to her when she felt nervous. Which, as much as she didn't like to admit it, was a lot of the time. Especially around new people.

Thums-Up was still whining and Kinjal put out his hand for the ball, which Kiya rolled back to her brother along the floor in the least furniture-damaging way possible.

"So what d'ya have against mermaids anyway?" Kinjal asked as he sent the tennis ball, and the dog, flying around the room again. Kiya wrinkled her nose as she noticed he was only wearing one sock. And it was dirty.

"Mermaids are gross," Kiya grumbled, not even sure if she believed it. "Women with sparkly tails who live under the sea? Come on, it's all magic and make-believe. So much less interesting than scientific facts. Plus, those mermaids probably smell like fish scales."

"Good one!" Her brother gave a loud snort. Which made Thums-Up zoom around in yipping excitement. "But seriously, what's your problem with magic? Do you have amnesia? Did you forget all the magic that happened to us only a couple weeks ago?"

Kiya didn't, of course, have amnesia. And she hadn't, of course, forgotten. Because, as her sometimes exasperated fourth-grade teacher, Mrs. Scott, could attest to, Kiya forgot very little. But what had happened to Kiya and Kinjal recently wasn't something she could share at school. Or tell Lola about. Or, really, tell anyone about.

Because only a few weeks ago, Kiya and her brother had ridden off on the backs of some flying pakkhiraj horses named Raat and Snowy across the multiverse to a place called the Kingdom Beyond Seven Oceans and Thirteen Rivers. The place their own parents were from. The place their own father was the rightful king of. They'd even discovered that their mother was a magical rakkhoshi and that they themselves had inherited some of her magical powers.

It was the sort of story that would make Mrs. Scott even more twitchy than she normally was, and definitely get Kiya sent to the principal's office. Which was not something that had ever happened to Kiya, of course, but she wasn't willing to start letting it happen now.

Kiya sighed, looking around their ordinary, normal living room in their ordinary, normal house in their ordinary, normal town. She felt bored. She felt itchy. She felt like she wanted to go on another adventure. Not that she wanted to admit any of that to her brother.

"Now that we're back in New Jersey, everything that happened seems like a dream." Kiya tried to keep the longing out of her voice but wasn't sure she succeeded.

"Well, it wasn't! Everything that happened was real!" Kinjal said through a mouthful of orange snacks. "We helped save the bees and the entire ecosystem of the pakkhiraj Sky Kingdom *and* the Kingdom Beyond. We fought the Serpent King Sesha and escaped his clutches! We discovered that we're a prince and princess, not to mention that you can make earthquakes and I can make water move!"

"All of that was pretty cool." Kiya glanced down at her ordinary-looking hands—hands that had done such extraordinary things.

"Pretty cool is right!" laughed Kinjal as he wrestled their wriggly dog, who was desperately trying to lick Cheeto crumbs off his face. He threw the ball high for an over-excited Thums-Up, who barked and leaped up for it, almost taking flight in her enthusiasm.

Of course, the other thing the twins had discovered was that Thums-Up wasn't really a dog at all, as she appeared to be, but actually a small pakkhiraj horse. Only, with the help of a magic spell, she could hide her rainbow-colored wings and appear like a normal Labrador retriever when she needed to. Which was all the time, naturally, while they were home in Parsippany, New Jersey.

"I just wish that Raat and Snowy would show up and ask us to help them with some mission," sighed Kiya.

"Hungry for another adventure?" Kinjal guessed.

MERMAIDS SMELL LIKE FISH SCALES

Kiya shook her head, annoyed at how quickly her brother had spotted the truth. "No," she lied. "Just so I don't have to go to this silly birthday party tomorrow!"

Little did Kiya know then that her wish was about to come true.

2

It's Raining Cheetos, Hallelujah

IN THE END, it wasn't Kinjal or Thums-Up but Kiya herself who broke the lamp.

"You're making orange dust fly all over the room!" she'd scolded her brother, standing up to put away the Cheetos. "Ma's going to kill you!"

But just as she grabbed the split-open and spilling bag, there was a loud bang from the backyard. She started, which made her lose her grip on the bag, making it rain Cheetos everywhere. Thums-Up, having lived so many years as a family dog, reacted in the way of most family dogs, running around and chomping on every piece of orange snack she could find. Even Kinjal, who sometimes acted more like the family dog than was probably good for him, was grabbing Cheetos with both hands and jamming them into his mouth.

"Stop that, Kinjal! Drop it, Thums-Up!" Kiya scolded, trying to wrestle a particularly large bunch of Cheetos from the dog's now orange-dusted mouth.

But in the wrestling process, Kiya had suddenly lost her balance, falling back into the side table and the lamp on it, which fell over with a terrible, splintering crash.

"Nice job, Dr. Perfecto!" Kinjal mocked.

"This is your fault! Now get Thums-Up into the back-yard!" Kiya yelled as she picked up shards of lamp. To her horror, she stepped into a big pile of fallen Cheetos and ground even more orange mess into the carpet. "I don't want her to get hurt by any broken pieces!"

Thums-Up, who had always seemed to understand more than a normal dog, ran to the back door almost before Kiya's words were out of her mouth. She barked and scratched at it, begging to be let out.

"I think there's somebody out there!" Kinjal was peering out the back window.

"Who somebody, like a burglar?" Kiya stopped mid-lamp-sweep-up, wishing she hadn't been so enthusiastic about convincing Ma and Baba they didn't need a sitter.

"No! Somebody like a pakkhiraj horse!" Kinjal swung open the door. "It's Raat and Snowy! They're back!"

"No way!" Kiya said, frantically trying to straighten up the room. Which was silly, because their flying horse friends were way too big to come into the house, so it wasn't like they would notice the mess inside. "You're imagining things!"

"Look for yourself, then!" Kinjal dashed out behind a now frantic Thums-Up.

"What are they doing here? It's barely dark!" Kiya ran out behind her brother, her heart pounding. She hated chaos, and between being alone for the first time, the Cheetos, the broken lamp, and the unplanned magical visitors, things were feeling pretty chaotic. "Someone's going to see them!"

But Kinjal didn't seem too worried about Lola's family, or anyone else in the neighborhood, catching sight of their pakkhiraj horse friends. And it's not like they were that easy to miss. They were huge, with giant wingspans, Raat all black and Snowy white. They wore jeweled harnesses, leg decorations, and headgear, but no saddles. And, as Kiya and Kinjal had discovered on their last adventure across the multiverse, Raat and Snowy were both the fiercest of fighters and the most loyal of friends.

Kinjal ran across the yard, throwing his arms around one horse's neck and then the other's. Thums-Up had unfurled her rainbow-colored wings and was doing zoomies around the yard that were half on the ground and half in the air.

Only, because she'd never been a terrific flier, she flew in crooked, sometimes upside-down circles.

"Raat! Snowy!" Kinjal practically yelled. "You're back!"

The horses neighed enthusiastically. "Hello, young foals!"

"Maybe we should all keep it down?" Kiya hissed, looking over the fence at Lola's family's yard. Luckily, no one was outside right now, but that didn't mean they wouldn't come out after hearing all this ruckus. And what they would say after seeing Raat, Snowy, and a now winged and flying-around-upside-down Thums-Up, Kiya had no idea.

"True, true, very true," Raat said in a lower voice, tossing his black mane. "These humans are primitive, backward creatures; who knows what they would do if they saw us."

"Kiya and Kinjal are human," Snowy sternly reminded his friend. "Well, partially, anyway."

"Yes, and look at them!" Raat huffed, stomping a giant hoof. "Covered in cheesy yellow dust! As I said before, primitive creatures!"

Kiya quickly tried to get the Cheeto dust off her hands

and arms, while Kinjal grinned with orange-toothed happiness. "Love you too, buddy!" he said to Raat.

"Your teeth are practically glowing in the dark!" The pakkhiraj snorted in laughter. "You look like the rakkhosh you are."

"Make up your mind, my giant, feathered friend," quipped Kinjal. "Am I a backward, primitive human or a backward, primitive rakkhosh?"

"Both!" answered Raat promptly, while Snowy said at the same time, "Enough of this, Raat! You know perfectly well our young friends are neither backward nor primitive!"

Thums-Up barked as she zipped by, flying upside down a few feet off the ground, her muzzle still a complete mess of Cheeto dust.

"Well, except that one, maybe," laughed Snowy.

Thums-Up whined, landing on the ground right side up. She turned her head this way and that, flapping her wings in confusion.

"Oh, you're a good girl." Kinjal gave her a scratch

between the ears. "Raat and Snowy are just teasing! They don't care if you're covered in Cheeto crumbs!"

They might not, but Kiya did. She tried her best to brush off Thums-Up's ears and muzzle, but when she tried to get the food out of her brother's hair, he shooed her away. Well, no one could say she hadn't tried.

3

Another Day, Another Crisis in the Kingdom

WHAT BRINGS YOU both here?" Kiya was still feeling nervous about who in the neighborhood might see their giant flying horse friends, but her razor-sharp mind was now also feeling nervous about what disaster could have brought their friends to visit unannounced. "Is everything all right in the Sky Kingdom? How is Princess Pakkhiraj?"

Princess Pakkhiraj lived on Sky Mountain in the heart of the Sky Kingdom, and was the leader of the flying horses. She was beautiful, wise, and, to be honest, sometimes a little scary because she was so powerful. In short, she was pretty awesome.

"The princess is doing well," said Raat.

"Then, is there something wrong with the bees again?" added Kinjal. "Did that blue champak we planted on Sky Mountain die or something?"

It was Princess Pakkhiraj who had asked for Kiya and Kinjal's help in repopulating the bees of the Sky Kingdom and the Kingdom Beyond Seven Oceans and Thirteen Rivers. Because, as Kiya and Kinjal had learned, bees dying meant plants, flowers, and animal populations dying too, since everything in the natural world was connected to everything else. Because their uncle, Raja Rontu, and his chief minister, Nakoo, couldn't be convinced to stop handing out free bee-killing pesticide throughout the kingdom, Kiya and Kinjal had used the magic of a rare blue champak flower to help bring the bees back.

Snowy tossed his white tail. "The blue champak flower you stole from the Undersea Serpent Kingdom is thriving— it continues to help keep the bees and nature in harmony!"

"Then, what's wrong?" prompted Kiya with a worried frown.

Raat and Snowy exchanged a look. "It's the water pari," Raat finally said. "They are getting sick. There is something wrong with their underwater homeland."

"Who are the water pari?" Kinjal wrinkled his nose. "I kind of remember Baba reading us stories about them from his book . . ."

"*Thakurmar Jhuli,*" Kiya supplied. It was an old book from the Kingdom Beyond that was full of both magic and stories. And even though Kiya kind of remembered hearing stories about the water pari too, she wasn't exactly sure what sort of creature they were.

ANOTHER DAY, ANOTHER CRISIS . . .

"I'm not surprised you have heard tales of the water pari from your father, Arko," Raat said with a snort.

"They take care of the undersea fish and animals," Snowy supplied in a bright voice. "They are a peaceful and gentle species."

Thums-Up zipped by, yipping a little. As if translating for her, Snowy continued, "And yes, as Thums-Up says, the water pari sing the most beautiful songs. About corals, starfish . . ."

"Seaweed, salt water," mumbled Raat under his breath. Kiya shot him a curious glance, and he looked quickly away without meeting her eye.

"But why are they getting sick?" Kinjal asked.

"We're not sure, which is why Princess Pakkhiraj suggested we bring you back to the kingdom." Raat stomped his giant hooves.

"Since you were able to save us all before—do what none of the rest of us could do." Snowy nuzzled first Kiya's head and then Kinjal's, which made them both smile.

"We would just have to leave a note for Ma and Baba." Kiya was already jumping ahead to practicalities, as usual.

"No, we don't have to leave a note," argued Kinjal. "We didn't last time."

"Last time, we were trying to rescue Thums-Up from being dognapped by the Great Blah!" Kiya snapped. It was true: Last time, Thums-Up had been stolen away by a giant fog creature operating under instructions from the evil King Sesha. "But we're not going to be that irresponsible now!"

Kinjal gave a big, fake yawn. "Okay, then, Dr. Boring!"

Kiya ignored her brother. But it was an effort. "We should take some supplies too."

"Are you sure you can even go, Kiya?" Kinjal said, his face all fake-sincere. "I mean, you do have that birthday party you've been looking forward to *sooo* much."

"The water pari cannot wait," Snowy said sternly. "They are very sick. And in grave danger of dying. As are all the creatures of the water world where they live, Pari-desh."

"Their wet, wet water world," added Raat with a visible shudder. "So much water in their world."

Kiya shot the black horse another curious look. "No, it's fine. I'll miss the party. No big deal. I'm happy to go help see what's wrong in Pari-desh."

"Well, at least this time, we're not galaxy-hopping in our pajamas." Kinjal pointed to the jeans, T-shirt, and hoodie he was wearing.

The last time they'd flown off with Raat and Snowy, they'd been wearing dinosaur and outer space pj's under raincoats and boots. It wasn't like either of the twins cared that much about what they were wearing usually, but that was a low fashion moment, even for them. The court ladies at their uncle's palace in the Kingdom Beyond had insisted on giving them both makeovers, which had not been Kiya's favorite part of the adventure.

"But I still don't understand." Kiya wrinkled her brows, trying to banish the memory of the fancy ladies and their hair-yanking brushes from her mind. "What are the water pari?"

"You have something like them in this dimension as well," said Raat. "What do they call them? They also live under the water, I think. Which is a decision I just can't understand."

"I remember!" burbled Snowy, jingling his jeweled harness. "The water pari in this dimension are called mawr-mads!"

After a moment's silence, Kinjal started to laugh so hard tears came to his eyes. "Wait, say that again, Snowy?" he asked.

"Mawr-mads?" Snowy said hesitantly. Thums-Up gave an enthusiastic bark.

Kiya groaned. "You don't mean *mermaids*?"

"Oh, yes!" agreed Snowy, rearing up with excitement. "Yes, that's right! Mermaids!"

4

Caring about Stuff Is Boring and
What Can You Do about Anything
Anyway?

THE FLIGHT ACROSS the multiverse was a long one.
Kiya and Kinjal had fallen asleep on Snowy's and Raat's backs
respectively, soothed by the gentle motion of their friends'
wings and the closeness of their beloved Thums-Up flying in
between the larger horses. They had been asleep for a good
while when, all of a sudden, both horses stopped mid-flight.

Kiya woke with a start. "What's the matter?" Night
had fallen gray and smoky over them, a thick and unusu-
ally heavy blanket of darkness that let through the light of
neither moon nor stars. The only light to see by was the
magical glow of Raat's and Snowy's shining harnesses.

"I feel strange," said Snowy in a faraway voice. "Tingly. Like nothing matters. Like nothing counts."

"I think we should turn back to New Jersey." Raat tossed his head, jingling his jeweled harness. "This mission is a bad idea. Have I mentioned before how much I hate getting wet?"

"What do you mean?" Kiya rubbed at her temples, wondering if she was dreaming. "I thought you said the mermaids were in danger. That they were near dying."

"Eh, the water pari will live," said Snowy with a thoughtless snapping of his giant teeth.

"Or not," added Raat with a snort. Kiya could swear she even saw the horse shrug his powerful shoulders. "Whatever."

"Whatever!" Kiya practically shouted in outrage. "How can you say that? Don't you remember that everything is connected to everything?"

Thums-Up gave a groaning bark and turned all the way upside down in midair, her tongue lolling crookedly out of her mouth.

Kinjal coughed. An odd, forced sound. "I think the horses are right," said her brother. "What's the point of risking our necks anyway? What can we do to help the water pari? We're just kids."

"Exactly," neighed Raat in agreement. "Kids who are not even that good at magic."

"Hey!" protested Kinjal, before letting out a strained laugh. "Well, I guess you're not wrong. I mean, we didn't even know about our water and land rakkhosh powers until a couple weeks ago!"

"And what's the point of such powers anyway?" Snowy turned around, heading back toward home. The night was growing thicker all around them. "Better just to forget you ever had them."

"Better to forget that your mother is a rakkhoshi!" agreed Raat.

"Or that your father is a crowned prince in exile!" said Snowy.

"Plus, did I mention how much I hate getting wet?" added Raat. "I don't think we're going to be able to save the water pari without getting wet. Better to just forget the whole thing."

"You're right." Kinjal's voice was faraway and dreamy. "What's the point of believing in magic and make-believe?"

That's when Kiya knew something was really wrong. Her brother was the last person ever to turn his back on the things that happened in his beloved stories. If she knew anything about Kinjal, it was that he believed in magic. His behavior was entirely illogical. And if there was one thing Kiya hated, it was situations that weren't logical.

"What are you all saying? Where is this coming from?" Kiya rubbed at her temples again. She felt a headache coming on, like someone was tightening a belt around her forehead. She shook her head, trying to think clearly.

"Didn't you want to go to your friend's birthday party?" asked Snowy. "Isn't that more important than a mission in a faraway place?"

"What's the point of helping creatures you don't even know?" added Raat. "Who live under the"—the horse gave a shudder—"water?"

"What have the water pari ever done for us?" asked Kinjal. "Let 'em figure it out themselves, I say! Anyway, wasn't it you who said that mermaids smell like fish scales?"

They were right, of course. Kiya had just been thinking about how much she hated mermaids, even in her own galaxy. Why, then, should she stick out her neck to help mermaids in some other dimension?

"Did you forget what happened last time?" asked her brother. "That Snake King Sesha almost killed us!"

Thums-Up yipped as if in agreement.

"You practically became serpent fodder!" said Snowy.

"Sesha almost made you into an appetizer, meal, and dessert all in one!" added Raat. "That said, I'm not sure how tasty you children would really be."

"Well, that's not necessary, Raat," Snowy said. "Just rude, in fact."

"I'm sure we'd be tasty!" argued Kinjal nonsensically.

"You're all right. Why should we risk ourselves for others?" Kiya felt the words come out of her mouth slowly, as if put there by another. The moment she said them, though, she felt disgusted at herself.

Kinjal made a choking noise. From her seat on Snowy's back, Kiya could see her brother let go of Raat's reins and clutch his own head, like his was hurting too.

"Wait, you don't mean that, Kiya," he finally said. "That's not like you at all. You would always risk yourself to help somebody else. You always try to solve problems whenever you can."

Snowy gave a hard snort. "This is true. You are very brave, Kiya."

"And very good at problem-solving," added Raat. "It entirely makes up for how untasty you probably are."

"I'm not brave." Again, the words came out of her mouth, but they didn't feel like they had started in Kiya's brain. "I hate solving problems."

As soon as she said this, though, Kiya knew what was happening. "It's the Great Blah!"

"No it's not!" Kinjal sounded confused again. "You're just making excuses because you know it's pointless to try to help others and don't want to admit it, Dr. Perfecto."

"Besides, I don't see the Great Blah," added Raat. "Might you need to get a new prescription on your glasses?"

"You're imagining things, Kiya," Snowy said gently. "There is no Great Blah here."

The blob-like smoke monster called the Great Blah was one of King Sesha's favorite tools of terror. On their last adventure, the Great Blah had not only made its way to New Jersey and kidnapped Thums-Up in a swirl of thick tornado-ish fog, but it had also tried twice more to harm them during the time they were in the Kingdom Beyond.

"It's changed, transformed somehow." Kiya spoke slowly, trying to work out the logic of what must be happening. Her brain felt like it was covered in a thick layer of Cheeto dust. "It doesn't look the same, but it's still here, changing the way we think."

Kinjal shook his head. "I do feel kind of weird.

Like there's a voice in my head telling me what to think and say."

"Exactly!" Kiya closed her eyes and concentrated on her own breathing like Baba had taught her, trying to be attentive to which thoughts were her own and trying to sweep away the Great Blah's cobwebs that had seeped into her brain. "It's the Great Blah telling us that nothing matters. It's what's telling us we can't do anything anyway, so why even try? It's what's telling us that trying to change things is pointless, boring."

"But that's not true!" Raat said with a loud whinny. He and Snowy both shook their manes, hard. "That's not our vibe at all! We don't believe any of that!"

"Let's turn around, team!" Snowy said. But even as the horses were trying to turn back around in mid-air, there came an evil cackling and spitting in the air all around them.

"You will never succeed!" the Great Blah hissed. "So why even try?"

Unable to see where the voice was coming from, Thums-Up began a frantic midair barking, whirling around and around, trying to find and bite their invisible enemy.

CARING ABOUT STUFF IS BORING . . .

"You're wrong!" shouted Kinjal into the air. "It's always worth trying! Man, this is just like in book twelve of *The Warrior Sloths* when the Chaos Monster does mind control on the King of the Sloths."

"You can't change anything!" the Great Blah hissed again. "No one cares!" But this time, its voice sounded fainter.

"Not true! When we work together, we can change things!" Kiya made her voice as strong and fearless as she could manage.

"And we do care!" Kinjal punched his fist into the air.

"We all care!" said Snowy and Raat.

And then all three pakkhiraj neighed and bucked, heading back in the direction of the Kingdom Beyond.

"Everything is connected to everything!" yelled Kiya, feeling sharp and fierce and like herself again.

"Everything is connected to everything!" answered her brother, Kinjal, his voice once again full of fun and magic.

5

It's Raining, It's Pouring

IT WAS RAINING when they got to the Sky Kingdom. Not the gentle, refreshing rain of early spring, or even the exciting, pounding rains of a summer storm. It was raining in kind of a thrumming, relentless, dull rhythm. It was the kind of rain that made the gray sky seem like it was crying. It was a strange, stinging rain that burned their skin where it touched them, like the water itself was trying to hurt them. Raat in particular seem horrified by the deluge, and for the rest of the journey kept up a low, muttering monologue about how much he hated to be wet.

When they had flown over the Kingdom Beyond, the ground below them had been colored in browns and grays. Even more trees had been cut down since their last visit, and more factories had been built everywhere with the horrible image of Minister Nakoo on them. The buildings rose like squat and fierce monsters from the ground, pumping their vile gray clouds of chemicals into the sky.

"Raja Rontu and Minister Nakoo have been busy," Kinjal said. "Are those all pesticide factories they've built down there?"

"Chemicals to kill bugs and make lawns green, yes," agreed Snowy.

"But also factories making raincoats and umbrellas and gum boots," said Raat, adding, "They are making a fortune out of this constant rain! I just wish they would make some pakkhiraj-sized raincoats already!"

As they approached Sky Mountain, Kiya could see the trees below were still green and lush, and could smell the flowers filling the air with their heavy, sweet scents. The buzz of bees was everywhere, to Kiya's great relief. But the winding river, which had once seemed to almost sing as it skipped along the rocks in its way, now looked, even from her perch way up in the air, sluggish and slow. The once sparkling blue waters were muddy, and, as they landed on Sky Mountain, Kiya wondered if she could smell a putrid stink coming from the waters below.

"This rain is the worst!" Kinjal pulled the hood of his sweatshirt up. "It feels evil!"

"Rain can't be evil!" Kiya argued, even as she zipped up her hoodie. "You're just wishing you had worn your old raincoat, like last time!"

Kinjal looked mournfully at his now wet, sneakered feet. "And my old rain boots!"

IT'S RAINING, IT'S POURING

Thums-Up, who normally liked to run around during rainstorms, trying to catch drops with her tongue, whined. She lifted her rainbow wings above her head in an attempt to protect herself from the weather.

"I can't believe it's still raining!" Snowy lifted his wings up too, like Thums-Up.

"It's been like this for weeks now." Raat snorted angrily at the falling raindrops like they had done him a personal wrong. "Have I told you young foals yet how much I hate being wet? I mean, the extra weight of flying with a wet coat, not to mention the way that Snowy here smells . . ."

"Speak for yourself!" Snowy retorted. "Neither of us can help smelling like wet horse!"

A bedraggled and drenched Thums-Up, who smelled like a combination of both wet horse and wet dog, whined in agreement.

Then there was a tooting of horns and flapping of wings, and from somewhere within the mountain itself emerged the pakkhiraj princess. Her multicolored wings were spread out wide around her and there were bells and flowers threaded through her beautiful mane. Her luminous eyes were wide and liquid, crinkling a little in a smile as she took the group in. Unlike the rest of them, however, she was not rain soaked, as there walked on either side of her two pakkhiraj attendants who held a beautifully decorated canopy over their leader's head.

"Welcome back to the Sky Kingdom, dear ones!" Princess Pakkhiraj's voice was like bells chiming, like clear waters dancing down a mountain. "Thank you for coming on such short notice!"

Kiya and Kinjal joined Raat, Snowy, and Thums-Up in making low bows to the princess of the flying horses.

"It's our honor," said Kinjal, pushing his soaked hair out of his eyes. It stuck up now even more than usual in crooked, funny spikes all over his head.

Thums-Up gave a sharp bark of happy agreement before violently shaking herself all over everyone.

Kiya, who always believed in getting right to the point of any situation, got right to the point. "What's wrong with the water pari, Princess?" She could feel the rain-water trickling from her hair down the back of her neck and wished there was a polite way to ask the princess if they could stand under her canopy.

"We're not sure what's wrong with the water pari," admitted Princess Pakkhiraj. "They are falling ill, one after another. As are the fish and other sea creatures whom they look after."

"Does it have anything to do with the evil rain?" Kinjal looked up mournfully. His nose was running a little, Kiya noticed, and he looked as cold as she felt.

"Or the color of the river?" Kiya pointed to the brownish river moving slowly down below the mountain even as she squelched from side to side in her now soaked sneakers.

The pakkhiraj horses all looked at each other curiously.

"I knew it," muttered Raat darkly. "I knew the rain was to blame. So much wetness falling from the sky can't be good."

"You didn't know it," argued Snowy. "You didn't even think of it until the children said so."

Raat gave a snort and a stomp of his hooves.

"Perhaps you are right, young ones," the princess finally said. "Everyone is very unhappy about these endless rains."

"Except the raincoat and umbrella factory people, those fellows are making a bundle," Snowy observed thoughtfully.

"Raja Rontu and Minister Nakoo are becoming richer with every raindrop," added Raat. "They'd probably be happy if it kept raining forever!"

"Well, let's go check it out, then—Pari-desh, I mean," Kiya said, getting to the point once again. She unzipped the backpack she'd brought with her. "I brought my chemistry kit with me so we can test the water."

Kinjal gave her an injured look. "I thought when you said you were packing essentials, you meant snacks and stuff."

Kiya rolled her eyes, tossing her brother a granola bar. When he opened his mouth, looking like he was going to ask her a question, she cut him off. "The answer is no, I didn't bring any Cheetos. I'm pretty sure you had plenty back at home."

Kinjal looked offended. "You can never have too many Cheetos."

Thums-Up whined as Kinjal slowly and sadly opened his granola bar, as if being forced to do so as punishment. He sighed, long and deep, before taking a big bite and chewing.

Kiya turned back to Princess Pakkhiraj. "Is there anything else we should know about the pari, Your Highness?"

"The problem is, they live under the water," began the princess.

Raat gave a low groan of distaste.

"Yes, in Pari-desh?" Kinjal said in a confused way. "We knew that."

"We both passed our swimming classes at the Y," Kiya volunteered. "I mean, my brother's backstroke isn't the best—"

"Hey, what about *your* butterfly?" interrupted Kinjal indignantly. "That's a total mess!"

"But we can definitely swim," concluded Kiya as if her brother had never spoken.

"They live *under* the water," repeated Princess Pakkhiraj. "Somewhere Kinjal, with his water rakkhosh powers, can go . . ."

"In your face, Dr. Perfecto!" Kinjal grinned triumphantly at his sister. "Not so perfect now, are you?"

"Whatever." Kiya rolled her eyes. But her brain was starting to compute what Princess Pakkhiraj was saying.

The princess continued, "But not you, my dear Kiya of the land clan. And certainly not any of us pakkhiraj."

No one spoke for a moment, and then the twins turned to stare at each other, both sets of brown eyes wide, all jokes forgotten. It wasn't like they hadn't been separated before. I mean, Kiya was interested in science, and Kinjal in stories, but beyond that, they liked different foods, TV programs, and even board games. In the second grade, they'd been put in separate classrooms, but that hadn't worked out for the best, so by the third grade their mother had convinced the school to put them back together again. But they'd never been separated like this—in such a definitive way—based on something that Kinjal could do and Kiya never could.

In the end, it was Kinjal who spoke. "So I have to go down to the mermaid homeland alone?" He didn't sound too happy about the thought.

"We can't go together?" asked Kiya. She was surprised to hear her own voice trembling a little.

Princess Pakkhiraj shook her mane, flapped her wings, and smiled. As she did so, Kiya noticed that a flower from the princess's mane had fallen at her feet. But when she picked up the flower from on top of her wet sneaker and tried to hand it back to the giant pakkhiraj horse, the princess laughed.

"That flower is for you, my dear," Princess Pakkhiraj said. "It is called an ichha-chapa."

It was a beautiful blossom shaped like a bugle, bright orange, with pink and red streaks along its many petals.

"Thank you." Kiya tucked the bloom into one of her braids. "It's beautiful."

"It is beautiful," agreed the princess, "but it is also magical. It is how you will accompany your brother to Paridesh." Leaning close to Kiya, she explained what Kiya was to do with the flower when they reached the edge of the ocean.

"But I'm not sure I understand." Kiya shook her head.

"You don't always have to understand everything," Kinjal said. "Not everything has a scientific explanation, you know."

IT'S RAINING, IT'S POURING

"I know that!" Kiya protested. "I don't need to know *how* the magical flower works, just how it will help me breathe under the water!"

But the princess of the pakkhiraj had already turned away and was whispering something to Thums-Up, who turned her head this way and that as if trying to comprehend. Kiya hoped it wasn't anything too important. She wasn't sure Thums-Up understood anything the princess was saying. Their pet was a sweetheart, but she wasn't exactly Albert Einstein.

And then they were off, flying away on the backs of Raat and Snowy toward Pari-desh. Only, Kiya had a bad feeling that she wouldn't enjoy the princess's magic gift.

6

A Fate Worse than Magic

"**B**UT WHEN WE went down to the Undersea Serpent Kingdom, Kinjal just parted the lake and I shook the land until the magic staircase appeared!" Kiya argued as they all stared at the magic flower in her hand.

They were standing at the shore of the ocean where the water pari lived. The rain had calmed to a gentle drizzle, but the sky was still gray and they were all still sticky and damp. Kiya's braids felt like ropes dragging at her scalp, and Kinjal's hair looked like a wet mop that had fainted, then kerplopped on his head. Even the two big pakkhiraj horses looked rough, with their manes and tails made heavy with rainwater. Only short-furred

Thums-Up didn't seem that much worse for the damp weather.

Kiya and Kinjal had dismounted Raat and Snowy, who were trying to convince Kiya to activate the princess's magic.

"The Serpent Kingdom just happens to be under the lake, but they don't live in the water," Snowy explained, not for the first time. "There was air to breathe down there. Not the same thing as this situation."

"We just needed to find a way through the water to Sesha's kingdom." Raat snorted forcefully, pushing air out through his giant nostrils. "But for whatever horrible reason, the pari live in the water—where none of us but Kinjal, with his water rakkhosh powers, can breathe."

Snowy snorted, giving his friend a *look*. Raat tossed his mane defensively. "You know how I feel about water."

"I just don't like that this is a magic spell that will only affect *me*," Kiya said in a low voice.

Snowy neighed. "Well, if that's all that's bothering you, the ichha-chapa flower's magic isn't just for you! It will also help Thums-Up travel under the water!"

"It will?" Kiya raised quizzical brows above her rain-splattered glasses, wishing Ma had agreed to let her try contacts already. "The princess didn't mention that to me!"

"But she did mention it to Thums-Up," said Raat. Thums-Up, who had been busy rolling around on the sand, getting good and dirty, now sat up and gave a sharp yip, as if in agreement. Then she shook herself hard, coating them all with wet sand.

"Thums-Up! Stop!" Kiya spat sand out of her mouth, while Kinjal wiped some out of his eyes.

"Raat and I are unfortunately too large for the magic to work on us," Snowy said sadly. "We will have to wait here on the shore for you."

"It's really very sad," agreed a way-too-happy-sounding Raat. "Very, very sad indeed."

Snowy rolled his eyes and whinnied.

Kiya sighed, staring out at the gray ocean with its unnaturally extra-foamy waves, like someone had piled pollution in the form of shaving cream on top of the water. The shoreline was dotted with beautiful coconut and palm trees, but instead of smelling like salt and sand, the sea air smelled seriously putrid. Maybe it was from the extra heapings of dead fish that were littering the beach right where the sand met the waves. Underneath the weird whipped-cream-like waves, the ocean itself seemed discolored. Instead of a gray-blue, it had streaks of brown and reddish goo in it.

"You don't have to be scared." Kinjal reached out to hold her hand. "This magic may feel like it's separating us, but it's actually so that we can go on this mission together."

"I'm not scared," Kiya mumbled, trying not to sound as grumpy as she felt but pretty sure she was failing. "And I know that."

Despite her words, she gave her brother's hand a tight squeeze back.

"So come on—get to it!" Kinjal pointed to the flower in her hand. "The water pari need our help and are probably getting sicker even as we stand here arguing!"

"Your brother is right." Snowy nipped her shoulder gently with his giant teeth.

"Better you than me," muttered Raat.

Kiya wiped her wet glasses with her wet shirt, which only succeeded in smearing the water around. She sighed. What would this magic flower do to her? Give her a shark head? Make her a fish? And could whatever the princess's magic did keep her safe in that nasty-looking water? She hated the feeling of not knowing. She hated the feeling of not understanding. She hated the feeling of not being in control at all times.

"You know, there's only one way to know what the princess's magic flower does," Kinjal said, as if reading her mind.

"Don't rush me," Kiya grumbled.

"The water pari can't wait," Kinjal reminded her. "Come on! It's like ripping off a Band-Aid. Just do it and get it over with."

"Of course that's what you would say, you chaos monster!" Kiya's nervousness was making her snippy. "Always rushing ahead without thinking things through."

"Well, what about you? Always overthinking things isn't good either! Sometimes, you have to just go for it!"

Kinjal argued. "Come on, Dr. Perfecto, time to embrace your inner chaotic good!"

Thums-Up yipped in agreement.

And so, Kiya took the leap. She did the thing she hated doing. She trusted in magic.

Princess Pakkhiraj had given Kiya very precise instructions. She was to stand in the ocean, at least knee-deep, before she began. And so Kiya took off her shoes and socks, lining them up neatly on the shore. Then she rolled up her jeans as far as they would go and stepped into the water. The cool waves lapped at her skin, the salt water making her pores tingle a little bit. But there was something about the repetitive rolling and crashing of the waves on the shoreline that made her feel immediately calmer. She also felt reassured by the presence of Kinjal and Thums-Up on either side of her in the water. Her brother and dog had come out with her into the waves, even as their friends Snowy and Raat stayed sadly on the shore. She waved to them, calling "Here goes nothing!"

She stared at the bugle-shaped ichha-chapa flower, with

its long stamen and thin petals. Then, holding the bloom up to her lips, Kiya blew gently through it, as Princess Pakkhiraj had told her to do.

She had expected nothing to happen, but the bugle flower made a sound, long and loud like an actual instrument.

"Whoa!" Kinjal looked as surprised as she felt. Thums-Up, who had become distracted by chasing a wave, looked up and barked in agreement.

The sound of the magical bugle blossom didn't fade away like a normal sound, but kept on bleating, loudly. On the wings of its reverberations came a shimmery, see-through magic that whirled around both Kiya and Thums-Up. It glittered and bobbed about them, making even Snowy and Raat, who were standing a few feet away, gasp in awe.

Kinjal's eyes widened as the magic mist swirled around his sister and dog-slash-pakkhiraj. Thums-Up was the first to become visible after the magic cleared from around her. When she emerged, she was wearing four little flippers on her feet—the kind divers wear—and a big, old-fashioned, clear, round bowling ball of a scuba helmet.

A FATE WORSE THAN MAGIC

Thums-Up whined, tail down, lifting her paws awkwardly the same sad way she did when Ma made her wear snow booties in the winter. Kinjal couldn't help but laugh. "It's okay, girl. Those flippers will help you swim and the helmet will let you breathe underwater!"

Thums-Up still didn't look too happy, but she stopped whining. That's when Kinjal turned to his sister. "Okay, magic mist," he said, "let's see Kiya's helmet and flippers!"

But as the magic cleared from around Kiya, it was clear that she wasn't going to get the same treatment as Thums-Up had. In fact, Princess Pakkhiraj's magic had a very different plan altogether in store for Kiya.

Kinjal didn't laugh right away. It took him a stunned minute to take in Kiya's new form. She had what could only be described as gills on her neck and a gentle webbing between her fingers. Except for that, she looked almost the same from the waist up—she was still wearing her braids, glasses, T-shirt, and hoodie. The problem was from the waist down. Because while Kiya was still standing up, instead of legs, she was standing on a green, sparkly, scaly tail!

When Kinjal started out-and-out guffawing, Kiya let out a piercing shriek. "Don't you dare laugh, you water rakkhosh dweeb! Don't you dare laugh!"

"I'm not laughing!" Kinjal wiped his eyes, trying to get a hold of himself. Caught up in the excitement, helmeted and flippered Thums-Up was dancing around the twins, yipping. Even Raat and Snowy seemed to be making noises that sounded suspiciously like laughter.

"That's great!" shouted Kiya. "Nothing happened to any of you! Even Thums-Up's just wearing a diving outfit!"

"Is this what they call irony?" Kinjal started laughing again, the waves lapping at his feet like they were laughing along. "Or is this what they call poetic?"

"Stop that! Stop that, you chaos monster!" yelled Kiya, looking down in horrified shock at her new bottom half. Then she wailed, "I can't believe I'm actually a mermaid!"

7

Under the Sea

"IT'S LIKE SOME kind of cruel joke!" wailed Kiya. Then she whirled on her brother, practically toppling over in the process. "Stop laughing already!"

"I'm not laughing." Kinjal snorted as he reached out to steady Kiya.

"Oh, get off me!" she shouted, shooing him away.

Kinjal was still laughing as he asked, "I was just wondering if you're going to dye your hair auburn or buy a clamshell bikini! Oh! Or maybe you might want to start a band with a lobster!"

"Stop that! Stop that! It's not funny!" Kiya wanted to stomp her feet, but instead, she just flopped her tail, almost losing her balance and falling over.

Kinjal caught her once again. He was still cracking up as he pointed at her back. "Did you notice you also have wings?"

Kiya looked over her shoulder to realize that yes, her brother was right: There were delicate wings emerging from her shoulder blades through two new slits in her hoodie. She tried to move the wings, experimentally, and found that she could flap them. She groaned.

"Great, I'm not only a mermaid, but a fairy too!" This was just her luck—she'd turned into not *one* but *two* goofy storybook characters, and both at the same time!

"Did we not tell you water pari have both tails and wings?" called Raat.

"Water pari really are wonderful creatures," added Snowy in an admiring voice. "Very magical."

"Magically delicious!" said Kinjal mischievously.

"I'm not a fan!" Kiya groaned again. She felt like she had steam coming out of her ears. Sensing her feelings, Thums-Up twined about her legs, rubbing her giant helmet head against Kiya's tail in what was obviously intended as a comforting gesture.

"You're being illogical, you know!" Kinjal finally said.

"How do you figure that?" Kiya demanded.

"Look, fighting your gift from the pakkhiraj princess isn't going to get you anywhere." Kinjal had finally stopped laughing and was looking at her in all seriousness. "Unless you have a better plan on how to breathe while we go down to Pari-desh?"

Kiya sighed, feeling the air whooshing weirdly through the new gills at her neck. "No other plan."

"So let's go?" Kinjal shooed Thums-Up deeper into the waterline. A bit more used to her flippers and helmet, their pet happily danced into the surf.

"Let's go," Kiya agreed in a resigned way as she waddled ungracefully behind them.

"Good luck!" said Snowy.

"Better you than me!" added Raat.

"We will be waiting right here!" they both called.

As they started traveling even farther down through the water, it took a minute for Kiya to get used to the tail and wings. Well, if we're being honest, more than a minute. It's not every day your average ten-year-old from New

UNDER THE SEA

Jersey is transformed into a water pari and sent to a magical underground realm. But Kiya Rajkumar was not your average ten-year-old, being the daughter of an exiled king and a revolutionary rakkhoshi. And so, it took her a small adjustment period, but she got the hang of it. Thums-Up also looked a bit nervous at first, but then was swimming down under the waves like a champ, her tongue lolling happily inside the diver's helmet.

In contrast, Kinjal seemed born for this mission. As Kiya and Thums-Up got their bearings, he did tricks, spinning and diving, flipping, doing underwater cartwheels and other tricks Kiya had no idea he could do.

"Where did you learn to do all that?" Kiya asked, amazed by her brother's abilities. "You never did any of that in swimming class!"

Her voice sounded a little distant and muffled under the water, but she was pleased to find that she could speak.

"I'm not sure!" Kinjal gloated. "But I never swam all the way under the water in swim class! It's pretty cool, isn't it?"

"Sure. Cool." Kiya was still struggling to use her tail to go in the way she wanted. "How is this so easy for you?"

"Dunno!" her brother admitted. "But there's something inside me that's just telling me I was meant to do this, meant to be here." Kinjal pointed to some of the brown streaks in the water through which they were swimming. "Even though I'm pretty sure this dirt and pollution isn't meant to be here."

Kinjal reached out to disentangle some brown-green algae that had gotten looped around Thums-Up's old-fashioned diver's helmet as well as her rainbow-colored pakkhiraj wings. Her voice muffled from inside the glass, Thums-Up barked her thanks.

It was dark and cold under the water. The heavy, thick stuff floating amid the seawater made swimming way harder than it ought to have been. As they made their way down, down, down, the fish and other creatures under the water looked startled to see such unusual sea life. The fish and other creatures that there were, that is. Kiya wasn't an expert on marine biology (she made a mental note to check out some books on the subject from the library the moment she got back home), but it seemed to her that there weren't enough fish swimming and quite a few floating upside down and sick or dead.

It was hard to say how long it took Kiya, Kinjal, and Thums-Up to get to the water-pari kingdom. The still strangeness of swimming this far under the surface had made Kiya lose all sense of time. As had her initial fear of being in such an unfamiliar place. And of course, the humiliation of having a sparkly tail and wings. But eventually, her scientific curiosity won out as she became fascinated with her new surroundings. She had always loved anything to do with outer space, and now Kiya realized that being underwater was a bit like swimming through a new multiverse. Being underwater was so different from being on land, such a rich and fascinating world unto itself. There were schools of fish swimming by, with some of their members looking a bit worse for wear—decaying fins and funny brown blotches on their otherwise silvery scales. A lot of the seaweed and other underwater plants also sported the same brown splotches on them. And as they got down to the bottom of the ocean floor, they noticed the shells of the scuttling crabs and lobsters all had the same weird spots.

"Something's wrong." Kinjal shook his head and rubbed his arms like he had goose bumps.

"No kidding. All these animals are sick." Kiya pointed to the splotchy undersea animals all around them.

"No, not that!" Kinjal said in alarm, pointing at something in the distance. *"That!"*

8

Undersea Villainy

COMING AT THEM through the water was a giant school of eels. Not just eels but green, glowing eels.

"That color!" Kiya said, swimming backward at the sight of so many beady-eyed and sharp-toothed animals heading right at them. "It's not natural! No regular eels look like that!"

"It's the same color as King Sesha's lightning-bolt magic!" Kinjal said as he looked around in panic. "They're coming right at us and there's nowhere to hide!"

Thums-Up whined, long and low, her voice echoing inside her glass helmet.

"You're right, Thums-Up!" Kiya pulled the dog behind

her. "A hiding spot doesn't matter anyway, because they've definitely seen us!"

"Oh, look!" sneered what appeared to be the head of the eel pack. Its teeth were wicked sharp and its attitude even sharper. "It's those little half-rakkhosh twins that King Sesha told us about!"

"So you've heard about us from the King of the Serpents?" Kinjal tried to laugh, but the sound was forced. "All good things, I hope?"

"Not the time for jokes, brother!" muttered Kiya.

The water swirled ominously around the eels as they surged forward, hemming them in, making it obvious they weren't going to let them swim past.

"Sesha told us that we should be on the lookout for you snotty-nosed land brats, since you tend to butt your noses in where you don't belong," hissed the eel.

"No butting! No butting here!" said Kinjal with an even more nervous-sounding laugh.

"Well, on a different note," Kiya said, realizing her brother wasn't making any headway with his attempts at jokes, "you know who we are, but who are you?"

"We're the Serpent King's special eel squadron!" announced the fish toothily. The swirling waters around the pack glowed green from their electricity. "Part of the new serpent storm surge."

"What's the serpent storm surge?" Kinjal asked as he treaded water.

"Well, that's for us to know and you losers to find out!" announced the eel in a nasty, oily way. "Sesha's got plans for this entire dimension that you're not going to believe until you see."

"Or maybe you won't have time to see them at all, because you'll be dead before you can even realize what's happening!" laughed another eel who sparkled all over with lime-green electricity.

Thums-Up unexpectedly lunged through the water, snapping at the rude eel. Unfortunately, she'd forgotten that she was wearing the glass ball on her head, which meant that her jaws just ineffectively bit down inside her diver's helmet.

The eels hooted and laughed, making Thums-Up even more upset. She thrashed about, making the water swirl around her. Kinjal reached out and tried to calm her down, finally just holding firmly on to her collar.

Kiya looked this way and that, hoping there would be someone around to help them, but unfortunately all the other undersea life had cleared out at the sign of the eel gang's approach. They were all alone, facing Sesha's hench-gang in a murky undersea environment—the eels' home turf.

"What do we do now?" Kinjal muttered out of the side

of his mouth. "I'm not sure these guys are going to let us go on our merry way anytime soon."

"We stall for time." Kiya swished her tail as she tried to think of a way out of this mess. "And fish for information."

"Fish for information," Kinjal mused. "I'd think you were trying to make a joke if you actually had a sense of humor."

"Not funny!" Kiya hissed. "As if this wasn't enough of a horrible situation!"

Thums-Up whined in warning. As the twins had been talking among themselves, the eels had been swimming ever closer and closer, grinning their weird toothy grins at them, writhing their bodies in ominous ways, all of them crackling with that glowing, green, frightening electricity.

Kinjal gulped, flexing his hands, clearly wondering what kind of underwater magic he could wield against the gang.

Kiya turned back to the eels, attempting to continue the fake-ly pleasant conversation from before. "So you said that Sesha told you about us—what did he say? I'm so curious!"

"He told us that if we were ever to find you, we should definitely make sure to kill you!" shouted the head eel, lunging forward toward them.

It tried to bite Thums-Up, but the undersea snake's sharp teeth slid harmlessly off her diver's helmet. In response to the attack, Thums-Up barked and then thwacked the eel hard across the face with one of her flippers.

"Leave her alone!" shouted Kinjal, sending a sonic beam of water toward the eels, which seemed to surprise him as much as the eel gang. The swirling undersea wave gathered half a dozen eels in its force and hurled them away. Kinjal's power, like his personality, was spontaneous and chaotic, but right now, chaos seemed like the way to go.

"How dare you?" snarled the head eel, its electric glow gleaming fiercely in the undersea darkness. It slithered through the water faster than Kiya could see. "You'll pay for that!"

But just as the eel was about to wrap its cruel, electricity-crackling form around Kinjal's neck, Kiya directed her hands downward, toward the ocean floor, hoping against hope that her powers would work underwater, and that, like her brother's powers, they could be effective in this crisis.

"Leave my brother alone too!" she shouted, directing her land energy with all the concentration she could muster. She wasn't chaotic or spontaneous like Kinjal, but she had other inner strengths. With all her might, Kiya called up the force of everything that was stable and true, solid and trustworthy.

At first, nothing seemed to happen. And the eels, who seemed to not just be cruel but have nasty senses of humor too, began to cackle in delight. "Oh, dat's so saaad! Poor weetle rakkhoshi doesn't know if she's a pari or a monster!" they jeered.

Kiya wanted to scream. Had the mermaid spell somehow stripped her of her own land-clan powers? But just as she was starting to panic, there arose a deep, guttural rumbling sound from the bottom of the ocean. It was a sound that changed the eels' laughter almost immediately to fright.

"What's that racket? What's going on?" The eels slithered around, trying to find the source of the sound. They bumped into each other, getting their bodies tangled and knotted together in their panic.

The force of the ocean-quake hit them more powerfully than a giant's punch. Pieces of the ocean floor slammed upward, scattering the entire gang into the far reaches of the dark waters. They shot back away from them in a pulling vortex of force.

Kiya let out a huge sigh of relief and gratitude. Her powers hadn't failed her, but had saved them all!

As the eels faded from their view, though, the leader's last, jeering call echoed through their ears. "Just wait until Sesha hears about thisssssssssssss!!!"

9

The Coral Castle

IT TOOK KIYA, Kinjal, and Thums-Up a while to recover from their eel attack. Kinjal kept mumbling, "Wow, that was a close call!" and rubbing at his arms. Thums-Up swam around and around in panic, and for a while even Kiya definitely felt like abandoning the mission and swimming straight up to the dry, safe land. But eventually, they shook off the experience.

"Nice magic, sis!" Kinjal punched her in the arm as they kept swimming down in search of Pari-desh.

"You didn't do so bad yourself!" Kiya said, returning the punch.

"What do you think this serpent storm surge is?" Kinjal treaded water for a second so he could look her in the face.

THE POISON WAVES

"Whatever it is, it doesn't sound like good news." Kiya sighed, stretching her neck. Her weird new gills made her jaw muscles ache. "But it sounds like Sesha's hired a whole bunch of new hench-creatures!"

"I don't think Princess Pakkhiraj knows about the serpent storm surge, or she would have told us!" Kinjal did an underwater back-somersault as he said this.

Kiya, who was barely used to the motions of her tail, looked at her brother's graceful movements with envy. "You're right, but let's figure out one crisis at a time, okay? We've got to find the water pari and figure out what's going on with them!"

Then, just when they'd been swimming down for what seemed like forever, they heard it. A beautiful, haunting singing. The sound filled the water around them, dancing about like it was something alive and full of joy. On hearing it, Thums-Up spun around in happiness, flapping her flippers and barking inside her helmet so that the inside surface of the glass steamed up.

The sound, they realized, was coming from a dimly glowing coral structure in front of them.

"Look! That must be the land of the water pari!" Kinjal exclaimed, pointing ahead.

As they swam closer, Kiya realized the coral structure was actually a beautiful and elaborately constructed palace, with towering walls decorated with shells and jewels, soaring towers, courtyards, and gardens. Most of the coral palace was sparkling with a glowing light that made it seem like it was a deep-sea sun. Only, like everything else in this underwater realm, great parts of the palace were splattered with brown sludge, pieces of the structure rotten and crumbling.

"Is there anybody here?" Kiya whispered, feeling instinctively like she shouldn't shout.

Of course, her brother had no such instincts. "Is there anybody here?" he shouted. As soon as he did so, the singing abruptly stopped. Thums-Up growled, disappointed, and stopped her underwater doggy ballet routine.

"Why did you do that?" Kiya flapped her wings in irritation. "What if there's something dangerous in there?"

"There's nothing dangerous in there," Kinjal scoffed. Then his face grew a bit more serious. "Well, probably, anyway."

"What if there is, though?" Kiya countered. "What if it's something like those awful eels—or worse?"

Inside her glass helmet, Thums-Up whined, swimming closer to Kiya.

Kiya put her arm around the dog's neck. "Well?"

Kinjal thought about it for a moment. "We're here to meet the water pari, who are all probably sick with whatever this stuff is that's making all the plants and animals sick down here in Pari-desh. And if the state of their palace

is anything to go by, they really do need our help! Also . . ."
He stopped.

"Also?" Kiya prompted.

"Also, if there is something dangerous in there, it's too late now," Kinjal said with an apologetic shrug.

"You really are a chaos monster," grumbled Kiya as the gates of the coral palace slowly creaked open, revealing the inhabitants inside.

"Sister! What are you doing out in the open?" cried

a water pari with a bright golden tail and golden wings, rushing through the water toward Kiya. "Are you lost? Are you hurt?"

The water pari patted at Kiya's hair, her face, her arms, her fins. Kiya realized with a start that the pari thought she was one of them.

"No, no!" Kiya held up her hands in protest even as her tail swished around, keeping her upright underwater. "You're wrong! I'm not one of your kind—I'm not a mermaid!"

But the golden-tailed water pari didn't seem to believe her. She laughed, a musical, bubbly sound that traveled through the water. "You have fins, a tail, and wings—what else can you be, sister?" Then the golden water pari's face got serious. "Are you ill? Has the sickness made you forget who you are?"

Kiya's face screwed up. She did not like confusion. It made her seriously uncomfortable. It's why she was such a bad liar. She took in a big breath, ready to set this water pari straight about why she wasn't, never would be, and definitely didn't want to ever be a mermaid. But before she could do so, Kinjal stepped in.

"My sister is just under a magic spell from Princess Pakkhiraj, who sent us. We're friends of hers," he explained. "She said that there's a terrible sickness here in Pari-desh."

"Oh! They are friends of Princess Pakkhiraj!" called the golden water pari, as if this friendship was all the introduction that the twins needed.

At the golden water pari's words, more mermaids came streaming out from behind her. The water pari who came out of the coral castle had tails and fins of all different colors. Not pastels, as most storybooks would have you believe, but the strong, vibrant hues of jewels—ruby, emerald, sapphire, and more. Their skin was brown, their hair dark and curly, their wings beating behind them to help them swim. They wore silk blouses and saris on their top halves, usually in colors that either matched or contrasted their beautiful tails. Despite their glowing beauty, most, if not all of them, had the signs of the weird splotchy disease that the twins had seen on all the other animals and plants of the underwater kingdom. The water pari swarmed around Kiya, Kinjal, and Thums-Up, all asking a million different questions at once. Who they were, how they had gotten there, why they weren't hiding inside, could they stop whatever was happening.

"One at a time, please!" Kiya raised her voice to be heard over the hubbub of musical mermaid voices.

"Well, that doesn't look good, does it?" Kinjal looked around them, where the water was swirling more red-brown than it had been a mere few moments ago.

Thums-Up whined in agreement, putting her flippered paws on both sides of her helmet.

"We must bring our guests inside! It is not safe out here!" burbled the golden-tailed water pari who had first greeted them. She looked at the red-brown waters and then around her as if searching for an attacker. "For multiple reasons."

10

The Mermaid Prime Minister

YOU KNOW ABOUT the eels? The ones calling themselves the serpent storm surge?" asked Kiya as she, her brother, and Thums-Up followed the mermaid in through the broad gates of the coral palace.

"Unfortunately, yes. That's why we've mostly been staying inside the coral palace," the mermaid explained. "We water pari have always been the caretakers of Pari-desh, keeping everyone and everything living together in harmony. We've never had such aggressive gangs marauding our waters."

"Do you know who they are? What they want?" Kinjal asked. "They said that Sesha sent them."

The golden mermaid gave a small shudder. "We do not speak that name here in Pari-desh," she said firmly. "He is far too unpleasant!"

"Not talking about unpleasant things doesn't make them disappear!" insisted Kiya.

But the water pari was clearly not having it. As if the twins had never mentioned the eels or Sesha at all, she began a stream of singsong chatter. Her name, she explained, was Shonali, and she was the democratically elected leader of the water pari.

"We don't believe in royalty," Shonali the mermaid explained matter-of-factly. "All that power just based on who your parents happen to be. We find it very distressing. Not to mention old-fashioned and unfair."

"My sister's not a big fan of tiaras and that kind of thing either," Kinjal said with a wicked grin in Kiya's direction.

Kiya ignored him. She turned curiously to Shonali. "So you only rule for a certain amount of time?"

"Absolutely!" Shonali swished her golden wings behind

her. "Term limits are an important part of how we rule. Then no one gets too used to being in power for too long."

"That makes a lot of sense," Kiya said, feeling impressed.

"Very cool," agreed Kinjal. "So you're the mermaid president!"

"The prime minister, actually," corrected Shonali.

"Well, nice to meet you, Madam Prime Minister!" Kiya laughed, putting her hands together in a respectful namaste.

Thums-Up barked happily, wagging her tail through the water.

But everybody's upbeat mood was soon squelched when they all swam together into the main hall of the water pari's coral palace. Because what had obviously once been a soaring hall of majestic beams and arches was now a makeshift hospital wing with cots everywhere filled with coughing, moaning water pari. Some had stained fins, others creeping red-brown sludge on their tails and hair, and many looked flushed and feverish.

Kinjal sucked in his breath. "So many of your kind are suffering because of the pollution in the water? Yikes.

Princess Pakkhiraj told us your people were sick, but this is horrible!"

Shonali tilted her head. "What is this word *pollution*? I don't know it."

"It means something that shouldn't be there, something dirty or causing disease." Kiya racked her brain for the best way to explain the idea. "It's when humans, usually, dump something into the air, water, or land that shouldn't be there—a chemical or trash or plastic—and it makes nature sick."

Shonali and her water-pari friends nodded sadly. "Yes, there is pollution in the water. And it is definitely making the water pari sick."

"We can see that. You guys look rough," Kinjal said, and Kiya elbowed him.

"Thanks, Captain Obvious," she muttered to her brother. "But a little unnecessary."

"What?" Kinjal rubbed his side. "I thought you liked it when I told the truth."

Shonali twisted up her face. "It is different than how you say. It is not people dumping things into the water. The pollution that is making everyone in the water sick is coming through the rain."

"The rain?" Kiya repeated, wrinkling her nose. "Are you sure?"

"We think so," Shonali said seriously. "Whenever we rise to the surface . . ."

"To sun yourself on the rocks?" interrupted Kinjal. "In pirate stories, mermaids are always rising to the surface to sun themselves on rocks."

"Yes," laughed Shonali. "As in your stories, we water pari do enjoy sunning ourselves on rocks."

"You probably need the vitamin D from the sun—something you don't get enough of way under the sea." Kiya gave her brother a superior look, muttering, "Science is so much better than stories."

"Sometimes, science and stories are just answering the same question in different ways," countered Kinjal.

"Well." Shonali cleared her throat, and the twins stopped fighting with embarrassed looks. "When we are on the surface sunning ourselves, the droplets falling from the sky burn our scales and fins. We used to think it was just a problem up at the surface, but now we see that the rain is—how do you say—polluting the water of the sea itself even way down here in Pari-desh."

As the twins talked with Shonali, some of the other water pari were playing with Thums-Up, throwing seaweed balls for her to fetch. The dog ran-slash-swam up and down the hall, fetching the ball and yipping happily. Even some of

the sick water pari lying in the cots sat up to watch the game with obvious pleasure. Then the water pari started singing again, which made Thums-Up join them with some ear-splitting howls.

It was hard to concentrate with all the noise, but Kiya bit her lip, thinking hard about what Shonali had said— about the rain that burned their scales and fins. It was horrible, absolutely horrible. But what could they do about it?

As if reading her mind, her brother tugged at her backpack. "We can't figure out how to help them until we figure out what's going on," he muttered.

"And how do we do that?" Kiya asked in frustration. The noise of the mermaids singing, not to mention Thums-Up joining them, was really a lot to deal with. It was hard to focus.

"Use that science kit you brought instead of bringing more snacks!" Kinjal said, triumphantly holding the kit up. How it had stayed dry, Kiya had no idea. "Isn't it you who always says every problem can be handled if you have all the facts and information possible?"

Kiya half frowned in her brother's direction. "I do always say that, but I had no idea you were listening."

"My silly sis, don't you know I'm always listening to you?" Kinjal laughed.

"That's very heartwarming," Kiya sniffed.

"Mostly it's because your voice is so loud and Ma won't let me get those noise-canceling headphones, even with my birthday money," Kinjal added.

Kiya rolled her eyes and punched him in the arm.

11

Rain, Rain, Go Away

KIYA TOOK THE science kit from her brother and placed it carefully on a flat pile of coral that looked a bit like a table. Fumbling with the test tubes and solutions, she gathered some of the ocean water and carefully checked it.

"What are you doing?" Shonali asked curiously as she and the other healthy water pari gathered around to peer over Kiya's shoulder.

Kinjal made a fake yawning noise. "Something boring and science-y."

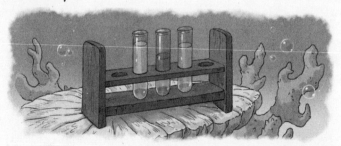

"You may think it's boring, but look at this!" Kiya's eyes glittered behind her glasses with the same enthusiasm she always felt when on the trail of a scientific discovery. "The pH of water is supposed to be neutral . . ."

"What is this *pH*?" Shonali asked, her golden wings flapping energetically behind her.

"I was about to ask the same question," Kinjal added.

"It's a way to measure, on a scale of zero to fourteen, the hydrogen ions in any solution," Kiya explained. Now that she had her science kit in her hands, she felt much better about being a mermaid. All she needed was a white lab coat that would fit over her water pari wings. The thought made her smile.

In the meantime, everyone around her was looking confused.

"Whoziwhatsit ions?" Kinjal scratched his head. "In English, please?"

"Or Bangla," added Shonali in a singsong voice. "But simpler, regardless?"

Thums-Up yipped, as if agreeing.

Kiya bit her lip, thinking for a minute before explaining.

"The chemical conditions of water are really important to understand how healthy, drinkable, and livable water is."

"Well, our water is certainly not healthy, drinkable, or livable right now!" Shonali exclaimed.

"That's exactly what my test shows," Kiya explained. "This water is way too acidic to be healthy."

"But the ocean is our home!" burst out a water pari with a jade-green tail.

"We have nowhere else to go!" agreed a water pari with a brilliant sapphire tail.

The other water pari babbled in agreement, their hair swirling, wings fluttering, sari ends and tails swishing behind them.

"Sisters! Sisters!" Shonali held out her hands, and the hall quieted down. "Please, our friends are here to help us! They surely have a plan to heal Pari-desh again!"

Kiya and Kinjal exchanged a look since both of them knew they most certainly did not have a plan. Even Thums-Up, who had been nudging half-heartedly at her seaweed ball, whined pitifully.

"The truth is, we don't actually have a plan," Kiya confessed. Even though she had more information and facts on her side, she didn't really know what they meant. How had the ocean become so acidic? Why? And how were they to even begin fixing it? She honestly had no idea.

There was an audible sigh of disappointment through the hall of the coral palace.

"You don't have a plan?" Shonali repeated in a quiet voice.

"Nah. No plan," said Kinjal in a weird, floaty voice. "But what does it matter anyway?"

"What did you say?" Shonali asked. "I thought you were going to help us do something about the pollution? The—how do you say—pH of the water?"

"We don't have a plan," repeated Kinjal slowly. His voice sounded heavy, like he had a cold, leaden and garbled. "We're just kids, after all. What can we do?"

"What are you saying?" Kiya hissed. She noticed he was rubbing his arm where some of the red-brown sludge had attached and caught on.

"I'm saying it's very sad the water pari are getting sick and Pari-desh is crumbling. I mean, you have marauding eels now threatening everyone they meet," Kinjal said in the same slow way. "But these problems are way too big for us. No matter what we do, they're just going to keep happening."

Shonali swam over and shook Kinjal, hard. Kiya tried to swim in between them. "Hey! Leave my brother alone!" she protested.

"No, this is a part of the pollution!" Shonali said, trying to wipe the sludge off Kinjal. "This numbness, this lack of caring. We have noticed it among some of our friends, the fishes and crabs and other animals."

"But not the pari?" Kiya asked. "It doesn't affect you?"

"Our magic protects us. Because we care so much—about not just ourselves, but all our friends here in Pari-desh," explained Shonali. "This is why you too are protected from this feeling of uncaring—you are protected by our water-pari magic."

That's when Kiya realized what was happening. "It's the Great Blah," she said, feeling that aha, lightbulb-above-the-head feeling, like she imagined a doctor might feel when diagnosing a rare disease. "It used to show up as a big tornado-like blob, but it's been showing up like this lately. Kind of invisible, but still able to enter your mind and make you feel like nothing matters."

As if confirming her statement, Kinjal drawled, "Who cares? Nothing matters anyway!" His eyes were unfocused with a faraway look to them. "We can't do anything to change what happens!"

"Stop that! It is dangerous not to care!" Shonali kept wiping off the sludge from Kinjal, now with Kiya's help. "It is terrible to feel you can't do anything!"

"Hey, lay off!" Kinjal protested. "You just don't like that I'm telling the truth! Nothing matters! You can't do anything about these big problems anyway!"

That's when Thums-Up swam over and used her tail to help clear away the rest of the sludge from Kinjal's skin.

Then Kinjal blinked, rubbing at his eyes. "I feel super weird."

"You should both go up to the surface now," Shonali said firmly. "Being in the polluted water is affecting your brother in a terrible way."

THE POISON WAVES

"The Great Blah has something to do with this poisonous rain," Kiya said. "Which means Sesha does too."

Kinjal shook his head, obviously thinking a bit more like himself again. He snapped his fingers. "I know what we have to do! We have to go stop Sesha!"

12

Good Plans Are Hard to Come Up With, All Right?

Y OU CAN'T STOP Sesha!" said Snowy and Raat in unison.

The twins had come back up to the surface of the ocean, after promising Shonali they would return soon. As soon as Kiya had blown once again into Princess Pakkhiraj's magic flower, her fins and scales had disappeared, and her legs returned to their normal human shape. So too had Thums-Up's flippers and helmet vanished, leaving her regular dog-slash-pakkhiraj-horse form. Reunited with Raat and Snowy, they were all now gathered on the beach, trying to make a plan.

"Do you not remember that Sesha tried to kill us?" Raat said with a fiery snort. "Like, dead?"

"And almost succeeded, might I add?" whinnied Snowy, pawing the sand.

Kiya thought back to the terrifying fight with the Serpent King in his underwater kingdom and shuddered. "Our friends are right: It's just too dangerous, Kinjal. And it's bound to fail!"

"So do you have a better plan to help Shonali and the water pari?" demanded her brother. "You brought your science kit all the way here instead of . . ."

"Don't say Cheetos!" Kiya warned, narrowing her eyes.

"Other necessary items," said Kinjal, "but you can't even tell what the test results mean!"

"That's—Not—I mean, but there's a perfectly . . ." Kiya stammered, then hung her head. Her brother was right. She had no idea what the low pH of the water actually meant, except what they already knew. Which was that the ocean water had become poisonous to the water pari and the other undersea creatures.

"I'm not blaming you." Kinjal had the grace to look guilty. "I mean, it's not like you're a real grown-up scientist or anything."

That stung. Kiya wanted more than anything to insist that she was as good a scientist as any grown-up in a white lab coat, but they both knew it wasn't true.

Kinjal's hair, which had been wet just moments ago, had dried magically now that he was on land. And unlike Kiya, he hadn't had to change form or shape. She frowned at him. She could still feel the tightness of the tail on her legs, the strange scratchiness of the scales and gills on her skin. She wondered if her whole identity as a scientist was like that mermaid tail—something that was make-believe, something to try on temporarily but not something that was truly hers.

Kiya sighed. "Instead of Sesha, maybe we should try and stop our uncle, Raja Rontu!"

"What good will that do?" asked Snowy gently.

"We don't know that this misfortune of the water pari has anything at all to do with Rontu," agreed Raat.

Thums-Up, happily free again without her helmet and fins, yipped in agreement.

This made Kiya feel even worse. In her bones, she knew that Raja Rontu, his minister Nakoo, and their pollution-spewing factories had something to do with the fate of the water pari, but she didn't know what or how. And it was the worst kind of scientist who made decisions based on hunches and not hard data and facts.

"The pakkhiraj are right: Rontu might not have anything to do with any of this!" said Kinjal, not bothering to dust the sticky sand from his feet before he put his socks and sneakers back on. "We know that the Great Blah has something to do with what's happening. And we know that Sesha has something to do with the Great Blah, so we just have to figure out a way *not* to almost get killed and go down and confront him. Plus, there's the whole issue of those terrible eels and whatever the serpent storm surge is."

"The not getting killed being the important part," Snowy said contemplatively.

"Indeed," agreed Raat.

"You were all very brave last time." Kiya looked at

both full-grown pakkhiraj, sparing a warm look for little Thums-Up too. "But we almost nearly didn't make it out. How are we going to pull that off again?"

"We're gonna need help, that's how." Kinjal rummaged around in Kiya's backpack, pulling out three apples. He tossed one each to the larger pakkhiraj, then started munching on the third, letting Thums-Up get bites between his own. His mouth full of apple, he said, "Hey, wait a minute. I know who can help us."

Annoyed he'd given everyone snacks except her, Kiya whirled on her brother. "Don't say it! Not her!"

"If you want to make it out alive after confronting Sesha, we've got to go see Queen Pinki first!" Kinjal said, naming the glamorous wife of Raja Rontu, the one who had plied them with mango juice and snacks on their last visit to the palace. "She knew our dad, and was his friend. And she really went out of her way to help us last time."

Kiya frowned. "I don't trust her as far as I can throw her. There is something seriously off about that queen lady."

"You're just weirded out because she was so glamorous," Kinjal scoffed. "But she's the one who helped us save the bees last time. If it wasn't for her telling us to find and replant that magical champak flower on Sky Mountain, the bees would have kept dying and all our friends in the Sky Kingdom and the Kingdom Beyond would have suffered!"

"Well, we did almost get killed by Sesha in the process of stealing that champak," said Raat thoughtfully, having gulped down his apple.

"Are you taking Kiya's side?" Kinjal turned to his friend accusatorily.

"There are no sides, I'm just pointing out facts," sniffed Raat.

Snowy looked doubtful. "Queen Pinki couldn't have known what would happen when we went down to the Undersea Kingdom of Serpents."

"Anyone who knew anything about Sesha, that nasty snake in the grass, would have known," Kiya argued.

"Well, do any of you have a better solution?" Kinjal asked in a frustrated way. "Queen Pinki helped us last time, so maybe she can help us this time too!"

Kiya broke down and dug out a granola bar from the

bag, jamming it into her mouth in a fit of hunger. The sweet taste of the chocolate chips spread through her mouth, making her brain cells feel perky again. "I guess if it hadn't been for Queen Pinki helping us escape through that secret tunnel, we would never have made it," she finally admitted.

Thums-Up gave a high-pitched bark.

"And that goofy birdbrain of a minister, Tuntuni," Kiya agreed. "You're right, Thums-Up."

Kinjal, Snowy, and Raat all stared at Kiya. "Don't tell me you can understand what Thums-Up's saying now?" Kinjal asked.

Kiya frowned, scratching her head. "I don't know, maybe."

"Interesting," murmured Raat.

"Very interesting," agreed Snowy.

"Magical," added Raat.

"Very magical," agreed Snowy. "Perhaps some of the leftover water-pari spell."

Thums-Up barked again and Kinjal gave his sister a curious look. "So? What did she say?"

Kiya made a face. "I don't know. I'm not magical, and

I definitely don't speak dog-slash-pakkhiraj! I just got over having that slimy, scaly tail, all right? Leave me alone!"

Kinjal laughed. "Not everything can be explained by science."

"You said it yourself: Science and stories are just different ways of explaining the same questions," Kiya sniffed.

"Not to interrupt this fascinating conversation, but do you think we might discuss the plan here, young ones?" Snowy said.

"We've got to find Queen Pinki!" said Kinjal with a triumphant grin at his sister.

"And get her to help us confront Sesha and find out what the heck is going on with the water pari," Kiya added with a sigh. "I guess."

13

Wanted for Crimes against the Kingdom

THE GROUP FLEW over more hacked-down forests and more factories, more gray and dull landscapes that had once been full of nature and life. That is, until they reached the outskirts of Raja Rontu's palace grounds. In the distance, they saw the beautiful forests surrounding the majestic palace with its soaring marble turrets. There was a sparkling lake, and beyond, mountains. And winding through those, one of the thirteen rivers for which the Kingdom Beyond Seven Oceans and Thirteen Rivers was named.

"Well, it doesn't look like our uncle was willing to cut down any of his own trees for factories," Kinjal said. "The palace grounds are still beautiful and the nature is still there!"

"But it does look like whatever's making the water pari sick is in his waters too. Look!" Kiya pointed down to where the edge of the lake was brown and littered with dead fish, and to the red-brown sludge marking one edge of the river.

"It's still beautiful, though!" Kinjal said.

Thums-Up barked in agreement. Only, because she was still not the strongest of fliers, the gesture sent her off in a midair spiral. When she stopped spinning, she was flying entirely upside down, her tongue lolling goofily out of her mouth.

"Do you think whatever's happening will hurt the nature here as well?" Snowy nudged Thums-Up with his nose so she started flying in the right direction again.

Kiya stroked Snowy's soft mane. "I'm sure it will. There's no part of nature that isn't interconnected."

Kinjal sighed. "As our baba always says, everything is connected to everything."

"But this place was once our home!" said Raat sadly. For both pakkhiraj had once served Arko, the twins' father, and his younger brothers before all those six elder princes had been banished into the multiverse and the youngest, Rontu, had taken sole power.

"We will get to the bottom of this, fix whatever's going on!" said Kinjal impulsively. "And who knows, maybe this place will be your home again!"

Kiya shot her brother a warning look. She didn't want to get their pakkhiraj friends' hopes up, or promise something that might not come true. I mean, could the twins stop something they didn't even understand? Besides which, for Raat and Snowy to once again be welcomed into the palace would mean their father coming back to the Kingdom

Beyond. But would their father actually leave New Jersey, and his somewhat successful gardening business, to challenge their uncle Rontu for the throne? They'd never talked about it with him, even after she and Kinjal had told their baba of their adventures. But it was an obvious question. Could their father do it? Would he? And more importantly, did Kiya even want him to? She had no interest in being a princess, that much she knew. Even less interest than she had had in being a mermaid!

As she was thinking all this, and before they even had a chance to land, they saw a familiar, tiny figure flying toward them through the blue sky.

"Tuntuni!" Kiya exclaimed as the small yellow bird landed on Snowy's back next to her. "How have you been?"

"We've missed you!" The wind was whipping around Kinjal and ruffling his already messy hair.

"What did the Raja say to the unwelcome twins?" Tuntuni burbled.

Since the bird was a known jokester, the twins and pakkhiraj all laughed. "I don't know, what did the Raja say to the unwelcome twins?" Kinjal asked finally.

"To make like a banana and split!" Tuni exclaimed in an agitated explosion of feathers.

"That doesn't really make sense," Kinjal began.

"Or, rather, it makes sense, but it's not particularly funny," Kiya added, always liking to be factual.

"You've got to scram! Vamoose! Shake a tail feather and cut loose!" shrieked the bird, who was a little prone to panic.

"Chill, Tuni!" Kinjal said with a laugh. "What's the problem?"

"That!" The minister bird pointed a wing down toward the ground. "That is the problem!"

"What are you pointing at?" Kiya squinted down in the direction the bird was indicating.

"No! Don't go down! I was given specific instructions not to let you go see those signs!" Tuntuni burbled nervously, ejecting multiple tail feathers in his agitation.

"Instructions?" Kinjal asked with a laugh. "By who? And besides, what signs?"

"Someone who thinks for some reason they can scare us!" Kiya said resolutely. "Raat, Snowy, dive down there. Let's see what's so scary on those signs!"

"No! I'm telling you! Don't fly any lower!" Tuni insisted with a squawk.

But at Kiya's instruction, Raat and Snowy dived down to get a better look at what Tuntuni was pointing to.

They were signs. Old-fashioned wanted signs, to be precise. And on those signs, underneath the words A FAKE PRINCE AND PRINCESS! IMPOSTORS AND THIEVES TRYING TO STEAL THE THRONE! WANTED FOR CRIMES AGAINST THE KINGDOM: DEAD, ALIVE, FILLETED, OR CHARBROILED! were three very familiar faces: Kinjal, Kiya, and Thums-Up!

"Up, you fools!" Tuni urged. "Fly up! Don't let the palace guards on the ground see you!"

"Why do they want to charbroil us?" Kinjal asked in a freaked-out voice. "And who puts a dog on a wanted poster? I mean, what did Thums-Up ever do to anyone?"

Thums-Up flew in a half circle of agreement.

"Our uncle puts us on a wanted-dead-or-alive poster and this is what you're worried about?" Kiya gulped even as Raat and Snowy followed Tuni's advice, flying higher into the sky and out of eyeshot of anyone on the palace grounds. "Did you see what else those posters said? That we were

impostors, usurpers trying to steal the throne! A fake princess and prince!"

"You, a princess? Pfft!" Kinjal laughed. "As if!"

"This isn't a laughing matter!" scolded Tuni with a snap of his little red beak. "Your uncle is serious! If any of you are caught by Rontu's guards, you're going straight into a gizzard stew!" Tuni gulped, dramatically putting a wing to his own neck. "Along with yours truly for helping you, probably!"

"Why *are* you helping, birdie?" Snowy asked suspiciously.

"Yes, how do we know you are not simply a spy for Rontu, here to lure us all into a trap?" Raat snorted.

"Because I haven't come just on my own!" Tuni admitted. "I'm here on special assignment!"

"Special assignment from who?" Kinjal asked.

"It's actually from *whom*," Kiya corrected him. "Which, from all the stories you read, I would have thought you knew. Although I guess *The Warrior Sloths* isn't really written with an eye to literary and grammatical correctness . . ."

"Don't insult *The Warrior Sloths*, Dr. Perfecto!" Kinjal protested, looking seriously hurt.

He really does love that stupid series, thought Kiya. "I'm just saying you could expand your reading horizons a little."

"Enough!" Raat roared.

"Shush! You're going to draw attention from the guards on the ground!" squawked Tuni.

"I just . . . you two fighting all the time!" Raat protested. "It's too much to bear!"

"It's a little stressful," agreed Snowy in a calmer voice.

Kiya and Kinjal exchanged a stricken look. "Sorry," they mumbled.

Thums-Up whined as Snowy sighed. "Am I the only one keeping my eye on the ball here? Who are you on assignment from, Tuni?" Then, with a glance at Kiya, the horse added, "Er, from whom, I mean?"

"Well, from Queen Pinki, of course!" burbled Tuni, puffing out his yellow chest in great pride.

14

Helicocrocs Are Really Bad News
(Plus Their Breath Stinks!)

THE MOMENT TUNI made that announcement, though, it became really clear that someone *had* spotted them from the ground. Two guard-shaped someones who looked mean, and very big. To make matters worse, they were riding giant, armored, flying alligator-beast things. Things with alligator-like bodies, steely wings, and swirling, mace-like tails. Things that neither twin had ever seen in the skies above New Jersey.

"Helicocrocs!" shouted Tuntuni, diving under Kiya's arm. "Fly faster, fools!"

The green-brown helicocrocs were close enough behind them that Kiya could smell their terrible, rancid breath and hear the *click-clack* of their jaws as they snapped at them in midair. She could hear the harsh voices of the guards and even imagined she could smell their heavy, perfumed moustache oil. Which, in combination with the breath of their helicocrocs, was making her want to gag.

"Stop! You impostors are wanted by the Raja Rontu for crimes against the kingdom!" shouted one of the guards, a man with huge muscles and an even huger moustache and turban. "You must land this instant in the name of the Raja!"

"You're mistaken! These aren't impostors!" shouted Raat even as Kinjal yelled out, "Oh yeah? Well, tell our uncle Rontu he's gross and he can go suck an egg!"

Both of the larger pakkhiraj horses groaned as the man started screaming at them, his moustache and weapon shaking in fury. The dank and dreary rain falling from the sky did little to hide his furious face.

"Kinjal, you chaos monster! Really?" Kiya snapped, turning back around on Snowy. "You had to say that?"

"What? Rontu *is* gross!" Kinjal yelled defensively. "I mean, what kind of a person puts out a wanted sign on their own niece and nephew?"

The guards chasing them didn't seem to care if the Raja was gross or not. "We know who you are!" shouted the other soldier as he aimed a very deadly looking bow and arrow in their direction. "Land right now or we will shoot you out of the sky!"

"I don't wanna be shot out of the sky!" Tuni burbled, his upset making the words come out in rhyme. "And be made into a mincemeat pie!"

"No one is making you into mincemeat pie!" Kiya assured the bird, petting him on his feathery head.

But her words were contradicted by the zooming arrow that came flying past their heads with a scary *zip!* She leaned down just in time, becoming almost flat against Snowy's mane, but could still hear the arrow go by her ear, way too close for comfort.

"That one was a warning shot!" yelled the guards, who were catching up to them. "The next one, we won't miss!"

"Thums-Up, to me!" yelled Raat, and Thums-Up dived into Kinjal's arms. She was too small to fly fast, and muscular Raat was strong enough to bear both Kinjal's and her weight.

"Evasive maneuvers now!" yelled Snowy. "Unless someone has a weapon I don't know about?"

"No weapons, I'm afraid!" answered Kiya. "Only snacks and a science kit!"

"Then evasive maneuvers it is!" Raat said, and muttered, "I hate those soldier guys almost as much as I hate this rain."

"What're evasive maneuvers?" shouted Kinjal, squeezing his dog-slash-pakkhiraj friend to his chest as she licked his ears and neck.

"This!" Snowy yelled as both he and Raat flew in 360-degree loop-the-loops.

"Whoa!!!!" shouted Kiya, Kinjal, and Tuni as Thums-Up gave out a loud and frightened bark.

"Hang on tight!" advised Raat, a little unnecessarily.

"Now you tell us!" Kiya was gripping on to Snowy's mane with both hands as Tuni dug his sharp little talons into her hoodie and shoulder. "Ouch, Tuni, lighten up!" she muttered even as she felt the granola bar she'd recently eaten trying to force its way up from her stomach.

"And fall down and go splat? No thanks!" Tuni screeched, digging in his claws even harder.

Kinjal, who loved roller coasters, was apparently having a great time from Raat's back. He held on to the horse's bejeweled collar with one hand and Thums-Up with the other. "Hey, Tuni!" he called, obviously trying to lighten the mood even as Raat and Snowy dived and pitched, rolled and zigzagged, trying to get them away from the soldiers' speeding arrows. "What do you give a sick bird?"

"Really, really not the time, brother!" yelled Kiya as Snowy practically flew upside down and she desperately tried to hold on.

"A *tweetment*, get it?" Kinjal laughed from his own practically upside-down perch. "Like a treatment, but for birds?"

Tuni, apparently forgetting his fear in his eagerness to top Kinjal's silly joke, flew up from Kiya's shoulder. "Hey, Kinjal, why does a flamingo lift up one leg?"

Kiya turned to look at the bird in fury. "That's right, you can fly! If you can fly, why were you hooking your talons into my shoulder that hard in the first place?"

Raat did another full loop-the-loop to escape from a whizzing arrow and Kinjal gave a whoop. "I don't know," he shouted, "why does a flamingo lift up one leg?"

Tuni acted like Kiya hadn't spoken and landed back

on her shoulder. "Because if it lifted up both legs, it would fall down!"

The arrows were zooming by now, along with the soldiers' shouts and warnings, which, clearly, no one was listening to. They were also yelling some very not-nice things about Kiya and Kinjal being a bunch of upstarts trying to take over the throne. Their mother would have been very upset to hear such rude words directed at them. Even writing this paragraph, I am upset by the meanness of those words.

Kiya, never one to let an inaccuracy go, shouted back. "I don't want to be a princess, but the fact of the matter is, Rontu is our uncle!"

"He stole the throne from our father, Arko, after sending him and all his other brothers into exile!" shouted Kinjal. "What a complete loser!"

"Liars!" yelled the soldiers, and the helicocrocs whirled their mace-like tails in agreement.

Thums-Up let out a frightened bark as one of the soldiers pulled out a match of some kind and sent a flaming arrow flying far too close to them for comfort! Kiya could feel the heat of the arrow as it flew by and barely missed singeing Snowy's mane!

"We can't outrun them forever!" Snowy sounded winded after all the flying maneuvers he was doing. "And now their arrows are on fire!"

"Now would be a really good time to bring out some magic!" Raat shouted. He too was heaving in big breaths and frothing a little at the mouth.

"Magic? What magic?" Kiya yelled. "I'm too far up from the ground to do any land magic."

"And I guess I could make it rain, except that it's already raining!" yelled Kinjal.

"Don't look at me! My only magic is my unbelievable sense of humor!" burbled Tuntuni.

Thums-Up barked, but it was unclear what she meant by it.

"Wait a minute!" Kiya fumbled in her backpack of supplies as an idea occurred to her. "I do have one piece of magic, I'm just not sure what it'll do!"

She held up the treasure she'd found, which was the old, tattered copy of the folktale book *Thakurmar Jhuli* from their father. The first time Kinjal had opened the book, back in New Jersey, it had acted like some kind of a magical beacon, calling both the Great Blah and Snowy and Raat to them. The second time they had opened the book, when they were trapped by the prejudiced General Ghora under Sky Lake, the magic pages had somehow helped them escape from under the waters. Now Kiya opened the book, unsure of what it would do.

"Here goes nothing!" she said, holding the ancient book above her head.

The power that emerged from their father's book of folktales filled the air with clarity and light. It made the rain stop, if only for a moment, and the sky brighten as if lit by the sun. The soldiers hid their eyes from the force of its power, as if it prevented them from seeing, which also meant the fire arrows stopped flying.

THE POISON WAVES

"This is our chance!" whinnied Raat. "Let's go!"

And the two horses flew ahead with all their might, leaving their confused pursuers behind. Kiya turned around on Snowy's back, holding out the book so it shone its shining light behind them, its stories a protective beacon shielding them from harm.

15

Poisonous Secrets and Secret Poisons

QUEEN PINKI WAS waiting for them in a secluded grove in the forest. She stood by the small stream winding its way through the ancient trees, just as glamorous as the last time they had seen her in the palace. She was in a gold embroidered silk sari, her nails long and hair lush, her eyes huge and dark, her mouth a deep red. Above her head, to protect her from the endless rain, she held a small and stylish little umbrella.

Pinki stopped smiling the moment she saw their dazed and exhausted expressions.

"The guards saw them?" she asked briefly as Tuntuni flew off Kiya's shoulder to land on hers.

"I told them not to fly so low!" Tuni wailed, losing some yellow tail feathers in his agitation. "It's not my fault, Queenie, you've gotta believe me."

"It's no one's fault but that awful Raja Rontu's! He's got to be stopped!" Kiya exclaimed as she dismounted the heaving and sweating Snowy's back.

"For real!" agreed Tuntuni, fluffing himself into a yellow ball on the Queen's shoulder.

Raat and Snowy were now both heaving and frothing a little at the mouth. They couldn't even say anything or acknowledge the Queen's presence, like they were too tired to even know where they were.

Kiya looked at both pakkhiraj with a worried expression. "Raat, Snowy, you two did a lot of intense flying back there, you're probably dehydrated! Why don't you go take a long drink from that stream?"

"Do you think that's a good idea?" began her brother, looking at the horses now too. They both really did look exhausted, like they were near to collapse.

"Dehydration is a dangerous thing! You can get really sick with your body chemicals all thrown off-balance if you don't drink enough water—we learned that in nutrition class!" Kiya said huffily as she directed both Snowy and Raat to the stream and encouraged both horses to drink their fill. She narrowed her eyes at her brother. "Or were you reading the *Warrior Sloths* books under your desk again during that lesson?"

"That's not it . . ." started Kinjal, but at Kiya's superior expression, he got defensive. "And so what if I was reading stories under my desk? Nutrition class is boring!"

"If you two are entirely done arguing?" said a smooth voice from behind them. Both of the twins started. It was Queen Pinki, tapping her toe impatiently on the ground.

Kinjal, who always thought a lot more about pleasantries than Kiya did, bowed low to the Queen. "Your Majesty, we apologize for our rudeness. It's nice to see you again."

But Queen Pinki didn't seem in the mood for niceness either. "I imagine it *is* very nice to see me," she said, giving Kinjal a brief but genuine enough smile. "But your sister is exactly right. This is unbelievable. That fiend of a husband of mine has got to be stopped! Putting the faces of children—Arko's children—on wanted posters!"

Kiya smiled, feeling pleased the Queen had agreed with her. Thums-Up, who for whatever reason had never been too fond of Queen Pinki, gave a low growl and kept her hackles up.

"Shush, girl," Kinjal said, scratching their upset pet between her rainbow-colored wings.

"There's something going on in the kingdom, something that's making all the water creatures, like the water pari, sick," Kiya said.

"We're not sure how or why, but the poison in the water has something to do with the Great Blah," said Kinjal. "And so, we figure, Sesha too."

Queen Pinki opened her mouth to respond, but Kiya jumped in to interrupt her.

"I also think it might have to do with the rain too." She gestured to the annoying, drizzly rain that now fell all the time from the dull gray sky. "I'm not sure how or why, but I have a feeling it's connected."

"A feeling?" Kinjal opened his eyes wide. "Since when does Dr. Facty-Facty Science Pants base her conclusions on *feelings*?"

Tuntuni gave a snorty laugh at this and Kiya shot him an angry look. To which the little bird shrugged. "Even you have to admit Dr. Facty-Facty Science Pants is a pretty funny name."

"I don't have to admit anything of the kind," Kiya snapped.

"Halt and desist, please!" The Queen rubbed at her temples with her long fingernails. "Your twinsy squibble squabbling is giving me a migraine!"

On her shoulder, Tuntuni imitated the gesture, rubbing his little yellow head with his wings.

"Sorry, Your Majesty," Kiya mumbled.

"Now, what were you even talking about?" Queen Pinki squinted at them like she'd totally lost the thread of the conversation. "Something about rain, and mermaids, and pants made of science?"

"Forget the science pants," said Kinjal with an apologetic look at his sister.

"We were talking about the water pari getting sick," Kiya began.

Queen Pinki made a dismissive gesture. "The ocean is a mysterious place," she said vaguely.

"But it's not just the ocean!" Kinjal pointed at the nearby river. "The waters here are turning brown too." His voice faded a little as he added, "And making the animals sick."

Kiya turned to look in the direction her brother was facing and saw their friends Raat and Snowy, who were both looking more ill than they had before, now that they had drunk their fill. She gasped. "Oh no! I told them to go drink from the river!"

As if on cue, Snowy turned a shade of green, spitting up a little. "I don't feel very well," the poor horse moaned.

"Neither do I," mumbled Raat, stumbling heavily to the right. Everyone gasped, startled to see the normally strong pakkhiraj looking so weak.

"That's what I was worried about before!" Kinjal said as both twins rushed over to their friends. "If the water can make the water pari sick, it can make the pakkhiraj sick too!"

Kiya felt like crying. Why hadn't she thought about the polluted water when she directed her friends to drink up? She'd been so worried about how hard they had flown, and how dehydrated they must be, she'd forgotten all about the poison in the waters!

"Raat, Snowy, I'm so sorry!" she apologized, stroking the necks of the ill horses. "I shouldn't have told you to drink from the stream!"

Thums-Up circled her larger pakkhiraj friends, comforting them by nuzzling their long faces with her own shorter one, winding in and out of their legs. But Raat and Snowy kept their heads bowed, groaning softly.

"You should get your friends back to their Princess Pakkhiraj as they do not look well," said Queen Pinki, squinting at the now coughing Raat in alarm. Kiya wasn't sure if the Queen was genuinely concerned for his health or just worried about catching whatever he had.

"But what did you want to talk to us about in the first place?" Kinjal asked. "Why did you send Tuntuni to find us?"

"I was seeking to warn you about the wanted signs, which you very cleverly flew down low enough to see, making my warning immaterial!" Queen Pinki's dark-lashed eyes flashed in irritation.

Even though she was angry, it was obvious the Queen had been trying to help them, which made Kiya feel even worse than she did already. "I've messed everything up. I'm the one who wanted to see the signs. And I'm the one who told the horses to drink from the stream. I'm sorry."

Kinjal patted her shoulder. "We all make mistakes," he said.

"Thanks," Kiya sniffed.

"Some of us just pretend that we're perfect, so when we make mistakes, it stings more," added Kinjal.

Kiya shoved his hand off her shoulder. "Okay, then, no thanks."

"Those giant horse types aren't looking too good," Tuntuni burbled.

And it was true: Snowy was pacing around and around in circles and Raat was wheezing and coughing while leaning hard against a tree. Thums-Up was so upset by her friends' illness, she kept running up to them and nudging them with her nose, then running back to the group, whining.

"We've got to get them back to the pakkhiraj princess," Kinjal said urgently. "She'll know what to do."

"But how do we get them home to Sky Mountain in this state?" Kiya's throat felt tight and her eyes hot with worry and shame. "It's not like they can fly."

"All right, fine!" snapped Queen Pinki, shutting her umbrella with a little *thwack* sound.

"All right, fine, what?" asked Kiya, trying to swallow down the lump in her throat.

"I'll do it! I'll send you to Sky Mountain!" the Queen said in a huffy tone that made Thums-Up bark. "But don't say I didn't warn you!"

"But how will you send us?" Kinjal asked.

"I don't think they're ready to know, Queenie!" said Tuntuni.

"Know what?" Kiya was feeling more and more confused by the second.

"This!" announced Queen Pinki. Then, murmuring a magic spell, she turned in a quick circle, changing from the glamorous but otherwise normally human-appearing queen she'd been into an even more glamorous but long-fanged, steely-taloned, and sharp-horned rakkhoshi!

16

A Rakkhoshi! No Joke! Seriously, a
Rakkhoshi!

YOU!" YELLED KINJAL even as Thums-Up went
absolutely bonkers barking.

"She's the rakkhoshi from the treasury! The one who
tried to kill Thums-Up last time!" Kiya shrieked.

"Well, *try to kill* is really a very extreme, very legal
term, if you think about it," Tuntuni began in a tone that he
must have thought was calming, but was really anything but.

"*Try to kill* is not an extreme term for what she did!"
Kinjal yelled.

"Since she actually did try to kill Thums-Up!" Kiya
added, even as she backed away herself, pulling her brother
alongside her.

"Oh, tomato, tomahto!" pish-poshed Tuni, waving a yellow wing.

"Ratatouille, shmatatouille!" said the Queen with a toothy grin at the bird.

"Gremolata, shmemolata," said Tuntuni in return.

Kiya got a weird feeling this was a word game they played often. "Stop that!" she yelled.

At the commotion, Snowy and Raat tried to put their heads up to see what was going on, but put them down again, sighing with weak sickness.

"Listen, I wasn't trying to kill your silly mutt-bird-horse thing!" Queen Pinki, now in her full rakkhoshi form, sneered, her long fangs glinting white over her ruby-red lips. She tossed her long curly locks over her shoulders like she was a model in some fancy fashion campaign. A fancy fashion campaign where the models had fangs, horns, and talons, that is.

"Thums-Up is not a mutt-bird-horse thing and she's not silly!" yelled Kinjal, holding their pet back from jumping on the Rakkhoshi Queen.

"And facts are facts; you did attack her!" Kiya was trembling from fear and rage.

"Just a little!" scoffed Queen Pinki, with a wrinkle of her nose. "A very petite, minor, pequeño little attack." The Queen let out a poof of air from her mouth, blowing away some hair that had fallen into her eyes.

"Just a little!" repeated an outraged Kinjal. "A pequeño attack?"

"She just said that," murmured Tuntuni. "What're you, like, an echo?"

"Were there any bite marks?" Queen Pinki asked, spreading her hands out, as if this was the most reasonable question in the world.

"Bite marks!" Kiya couldn't believe what she was hearing. "Are you serious?"

"If there are no bite marks," Tuni said in a fake-lawyer-y way, "then you must begin at the start."

"What does that even mean?" yelled Kinjal.

"Honestly, I'm not sure," confessed Tuni, scratching his feathery chin with a wing. "It's not like I've been to law school, you know. The entrance exams aren't exactly easy, and the admissions policies are definitely prejudiced against birds."

Thums-Up apparently agreed with the law school admissions officers, because on hearing this, she growled, snapping at Tuni, who flew up to a higher branch, out of the reach of her teeth.

"You all are in a huff over absolutely nothing," the Rakkhoshi Queen was explaining in an over-patient way. She rubbed her chest in a gesture that Kiya remembered, like she was hurting from heartburn. "And to be fair, at the time I semi-attacked your little crookedly flying oddball companion here, I didn't know you were Arko's children!"

"How is that even an excuse?" Kiya demanded. "You shouldn't be attacking her anyway!"

Kinjal placed his hands over Thums-Up's ears. "Also, don't insult her flying! She's very sensitive about that!"

"Darling, I never offer excuses," drawled the Queen, ignoring Kinjal's comment. She let out an elegant little burp. "Just explanations."

"Well, I'm not going to let you hurt Thums-Up, or anyone, again!" announced Kiya boldly. Without even thinking about it, she slammed her hands onto the ground, making the land quake all around Queen Pinki's feet. The glamorous rakkhoshi stumbled, nearly falling down.

The Queen's eyes flashed hot and fiery. "Well, aren't you a little precocious self-starter!" she sneered, sending a smoke bomb from her hands in Kiya's direction. Kiya fell backward onto the ground, coughing.

"Don't hurt my sister!" shouted Kinjal, blasting a rain cloud from his hands toward the Queen. His waters cut through the smoke, and would have drenched the rakkhoshi if she hadn't made the cloud disappear with a snap of her fingers.

"A-plus for effort, young ding-a-lings," Queen Pinki said, impatience ringing in her voice. "But I think there's an important thing you're both forgetting."

"What's that?" Kinjal asked, while at the same time Kiya yelled, "We're not ding-a-lings!"

Breaking free of Kinjal's grasp suddenly, Thums-Up lunged at the rakkhoshi. "No!" Kinjal yelled, reaching for the pup-slash-pakkhiraj but missing her collar as she flew past.

Before Thums-Up reached her, the Queen waved a

fireball from her hands, trapping a barking and frightened Thums-Up behind a wall of flames.

"Let her go!" shouted Kiya, ready to make the land shake again. "You monster!"

"Oh, for all the ignorant baby rakkhosh in the world, I had to get saddled with you two!" groaned the Queen, as if to herself. "If you look carefully, you will see your pet is perfectly safe. Just trapped for the moment. And if you remember, you two are monsters just like me!"

And as Kiya and Kinjal looked, they realized Queen Pinki was telling the truth. She had trapped Thums-Up behind a wall of flames that didn't seem to hurt their pet at all. Of course, that didn't help calm terrified Thums-Up, who was barking now at a shrill, high, frightened pitch.

"I'll even be so gracious as to let her go if she promises to keep her teeth and fleas to herself, thank you very much!" the rakkhoshi drawled, tossing her luxurious hair over her horns once again.

From behind the fence of flames, Thums-Up growled and barked some more.

"She says she doesn't have fleas!" Kiya translated.

Kinjal gave her a funny look but said nothing. "Yes, please let her go now. Thums-Up promises to behave herself."

"I'll be the judge of that." But with a snort, Queen Pinki released Thums-Up from her fence. The dog-slash-pakkhiraj growled, her hackles up, but didn't approach the Queen again.

"I think you two have gotten a little distracted from the main plot point at hand," Queen Pinki said, with a pointed look in Raat and Snowy's direction.

17

Eureka! But Also, Oh Well

WITH A START, Kiya realized she had forgotten all about their sick friends, who now looked so dazed and out of it, they were barely conscious. She gulped, trying to refocus on what was important. "You said you would help us get our friends to Snow Mountain, so the pakkhiraj princess can heal them."

"But how can you do that? They're huge!" Kinjal said.

Kiya thought longingly of the horse trailers she'd seen on the New Jersey Turnpike. But she guessed no such things existed here in the Kingdom Beyond, where she'd never seen a car, let alone a tractor trailer.

"You're forgetting that I'm a very powerful rakkhoshi."

The Queen clicked her fangs with indulgent patience. "I will simply magic you there."

"Why would you do that?" Kiya asked.

"Because I'm really on your side. And I know, perfectly well, the meaning of your father's favorite saying," Queen Pinki said, a twinkle in her eye.

"Everything is connected to everything?" Kinjal asked.

"Exactly." The Queen waved her talons at them. "Who do you think taught him that little ditty?"

Kiya and Kinjal exchanged half-horrified, half-shocked looks. The Queen and their father really had been friends!

"All right, go gather by your puking horsies. Make sure you all have a tight grip on each other!" the Queen advised. Then, with a grimace, she rubbed at her chest again. "Oof, this acid reflux is absolutely horrible."

Kiya had walked away, halfway to Raat and Snowy, when the Queen's words registered in her mind. She turned around, her eyes wide as she felt the gears in her scientific brain whirring to life. "Wait, what did you say?"

"To gather your little horse-bird-creature friends?" the

Rakkhoshi Queen drawled, pointing with one talon in the direction of Raat and Snowy even as she continued rubbing at her chest.

"No, not that." Kiya knew she was on the verge of a breakthrough, like the word *eureka!* was about to pop up in a bubble above her brain. "The thing about your reflux."

"My acid reflux?" Pinki burbled, pounding her chest a little with a fist. "Eh, it's just a little side effect of my fire-breathing magic."

"That's it!" whispered Kiya to herself, closing her eyes and trying to see the page of her science textbook in her mind. It was a neat trick her memory sometimes could do, re-create the image of something she'd read in her head, like she was seeing it all over again.

"What's up?" Kinjal was looking at her like he was worried she'd drunk a bunch of poisoned water too.

"It's the answer to the low pH of the ocean water. I had a hunch it had something to do with all this endless rain, and I think I'm right," Kiya said slowly. "Low pH is also called acidic. And I think this kind of pollution is called acid rain.

It's caused by cars and factories sending chemicals into the air that mix inside rain clouds and fall back down to the ground as sulfuric and nitric acid."

Kinjal wrinkled his nose. "Whatever it is, it doesn't sound good."

"It's not!" Kiya agreed. "But that means my hunch was right! And more importantly, we've got to change our plans! We've got to go talk to the Raja and get him to shut down the factories!"

"And he's just going to—what—agree to do that because we ask nicely?" Kinjal looked at her like she'd lost all sense of reality. "Do you not remember what happened last time we tried to ask him something like that? We got chased out of the kingdom by some mean dudes with some seriously sharp swords!"

"But it's the answer! His factories are polluting the air— we saw that!" Kiya insisted. "And then that pollution is getting absorbed and falling down to the groundwater in the form of acid rain!"

The Queen let out a giant fiery belch. "Have you

forgotten something? That my darling husband has put an actual bounty on your actual heads? You can't just waltz into the palace and speak to him! You'll get smooshed into aloo chops before you enter the front door!"

"Out of the question!" agreed Tuntuni. "Though some potato chops right about now would be awfully tasty. Mmm, with some mint chutney on the side."

Kiya glared at Tuni. Raat and Snowy let out low moans, and Thums-Up whined in sympathy.

"The fact that your hunch was right doesn't matter now anyway!" Kinjal said urgently. "We've got to get Raat and Snowy to Princess Pakkhiraj."

Kiya sighed. Her brother was right, of course. They had to help their friends. But it was frustrating too, because she'd figured out the answer of why the rains were connected to the pollution of the oceans, and how to stop what was happening to the water pari.

"Raja Rontu and his minister Nakoo are making more factories all around the Kingdom Beyond every day!" Kiya said in a small voice. "It is a scientific fact that factory pollution makes acid rain, which is what's making the water pari sick."

"Rontu and Nakoo will never shut down those factories," the Queen said with a dismissive gesture, like she was shooing away a fly.

"Never," echoed Tuntuni from her shoulder, imitating the same gesture.

Kiya wanted to shout that there was always a way. That negativity was a bad look. That with hard work, and energy, and vision, they could achieve anything. But Kinjal squeezed her arm tight. "We'll figure it all out when Raat and Snowy are better."

Kiya nodded. Now they had to focus on her sick friends. "Let's get them home."

Kiya was petting their dear pakkhiraj friends, who could barely stand at this point. She supported Raat around the neck with her arms as Kinjal did the same for Snowy. Thums-Up leaned hard against their legs as they all bunched together, waiting to be beamed away, or whatever the Rakkhoshi Queen was about to do to them.

"Tell Princess Pakkhiraj I send my greetings," called Queen Pinki. "She's really far too earnest for my tastes, but I do respect her style. All that fierce anger to mix up the gentle goofiness; tell her I approve."

Kinjal raised his eyebrows. "Um, okay."

"Now, is everyone ready to be magically transported?" Tuntuni burbled, like he was the conductor on some kind of magical amusement park ride. "Hold on to your socks!"

"You too, birdbrain," Pinki said firmly, transferring Minister Tuni from her own shoulder to Kiya's.

"Me? Why me, Queenie?" protested the bird. "I don't wanna go on another adventure. There are never very good snacks on adventures!"

"How about this?" Kinjal offered, holding out a granola bar.

Tuni sniffed but, Kiya noticed, still scarfed down a bit of the nutty bar. "It's subpar to the gourmet five-course meals I'm accustomed to eating at the palace, but I'll make an exception," muttered the bird through a full beak of food.

"All right, kiddies, say the magic words!" singsonged the Queen.

"Abracadabra?" asked Kiya.

"Hocus-pocus?" guessed Kinjal.

"No, you ninnies!" fumed Pinki, two plumes of steam coming out of her nostrils. "Honestly, when I next see him, I'm going to have to give Arko a piece of my mind about the way he raised you two goofballs!"

"We know, we know!" Kiya smiled. And then, in unison

with her brother, she said the words that Pinki and her father had once shared. "Everything is connected to everything!"

And then, with a fiery snap of her fingers, Queen Pinki sent them out of the grove and back to Sky Mountain.

18

Back to Sky Mountain

PRINCESS PAKKHIRAJ BUCKED and neighed in alarm when she saw the state of Raat and Snowy. The black and white pakkhiraj horses were drooping with exhaustion, their eyes unfocused and steps unsteady. Their feathers were molting and neither was able to speak coherently anymore, only drooling long streams of fuzzy stuff from their mouths.

"General Ghora, take them immediately to the infirmary!" she ordered the red-armored General, the same horse who had once imprisoned Kiya and Kinjal under Sky Lake.

"My princess, I cannot leave you with these beast children! They may be dangerous!" General Ghora gave a snort through her nostrils. "And that dirty bird—what diseases might it be carrying?!"

"Hey, that's way uncool!" protested Tuntuni. "I take my vitamins! I'm not carrying any diseases!"

Kiya petted the yellow bird's ruffled feathers. "We know you're not," she soothed.

"And we are *not* beasts! We're rakkhosh like our mom!" Kinjal said huffily.

"How dare you insult my guests, General Ghora!" Princess Pakkhiraj whirled on the General, raising her wings and becoming a larger, fiercer, glowing version of her normal self. When she spoke, her voice echoed strangely off the cliffs of Sky Mountain, across Sky Valley, and probably through every corner of the pakkhiraj homeland of Sky Kingdom. "I have warned you before about this prejudice you have against anyone different than yourself! You serve our people well, but this hatred for others is like a poison of the mind as powerful as the poison that is sickening our waters!"

Kiya thought of how untrusting they had just been of Queen Pinki, when they discovered she too was a rakkhoshi.

But that wasn't like General Ghora's prejudice, or was it? I mean, Pinki had tried to attack Thums-Up in the treasury when they first met. Hadn't she? Or were she and Kinjal just acting under the same stereotypes about rakkhosh that General Ghora was, even though they themselves were part rakkhosh?

"I apologize, Your Highness. I am just worried about your well-being in these troubled times." Even though her words were kind and gentle, the look that the General shot Kiya and Kinjal was anything but kind or gentle. She even snapped her teeth menacingly at Tuntuni when the princess wasn't looking. In response, Tuni blew a wet raspberry in the General's direction. Kiya knew she should scold Tuni for his behavior, but decided to let it go.

Raat gave a low moan, and Kiya's logical mind focused on the issue at hand. "We forgive you, General. Now, please, make sure you look after our friends; they are very sick!"

General Ghora looked like she wanted to say something else, but Princess Pakkhiraj cut her off with an impatient wave of one of her giant wings. "Enough! Do as my dear young friend says and look after Raat and Snowy immediately!"

As General Ghora led Raat and Snowy away, Princess Pakkhiraj sighed. "I'm so sorry about that." She made herself smaller again—although her normal size was still pretty big—and smiled gently at the twins. "There were once terrible wars between the pakkhiraj and the rakkhosh, but it is no excuse for keeping such prejudices alive."

Kiya wanted to ask more about the wars, but Kinjal spoke first. "We just want to make sure Raat and Snowy are all right."

"We can heal them, I believe, with our community's magic," Princess Pakkhiraj said reassuringly.

Tuni chose this moment to fly from Kiya's shoulder to the princess's wing. "Your Highness, what do you call an owl who can do magic?" he asked pertly.

"This is probably not the time, Tuni," Kiya muttered.

"I don't know, my small friend," said the princess gamely. "What do you call an owl who can do magic?"

"A Hoo-dini," announced Tuni, rolling in laughter and clutching at his yellow belly.

Princess Pakkhiraj frowned. "I'm afraid I don't understand."

"Houdini was the name of a famous magician from our corner of the multiverse," said Kinjal. He frowned at Tuni. "Even though I'm not sure how Tuni knows about him."

"Here's another one," said Tuni, obviously on a roll. "How many magicians does it take to do magic?"

"Tuni, seriously, there are more important things to worry about right now." Kiya couldn't believe Queen Pinki had sent the silly bird along. Was this supposed to be helpful?

"I don't know, Tuni, how many magicians does it take?" asked Kinjal.

"Just one will do the trick!" laughed the yellow bird, flying around their heads in a loop-the-loop of laughter. Thums-Up jumped up, barking, excited by Tuni's flying motion, but the bird stayed out of the reach of her sharp teeth.

Princess Pakkhiraj smiled indulgently at the pair of animals. "Why don't you two go to the infirmary with Raat and Snowy, keep their spirits up?"

As the small bird and dog-slash-pakkhiraj danced off, the princess turned to the twins. "There is always time for laughter, my friends, even in challenging times. Especially in the most difficult moments, joy is how we make it through."

Kiya knew the princess was trying to teach her a lesson but couldn't help but ask impatiently, "You are healing Raat and Snowy; what about the next person or animal who drinks from a stream, or lake, or river? What happens when everyone starts getting ill from this endless acid rain? Can your magic heal the poison in the waters?"

Kiya thought Kinjal might get on her case for being so serious, but he was obviously worrying about the acid rain too. "And then there are the water pari," he said. "It's getting near impossible to live in Pari-desh."

The twins explained to Princess Pakkhiraj what they'd seen under the water in the land of the water pari, how so many of their people were sick, not to mention the dead and dying fish and other undersea creatures they'd seen. They told her about their strange encounter with the eels who claimed they were working for Sesha. They told her about Raja Rontu's wanted posters, and Queen Pinki's secret identity. Finally, they told her what Kiya had figured out about the rain itself and how it was polluting the waters.

"Queen Pinki doesn't think that the Raja can be convinced to shut down his factories," Kinjal explained.

"But she sends her greetings to you," Kiya added.

Princess Pakkhiraj made a funny snorting noise at this. Kiya wasn't sure what to make of it. "He doesn't know what she is, of course," the leader of the pakkhiraj horses finally said. "Her husband, Rontu, thinks she's just a regular human being."

Kiya frowned. She wasn't sure at all what she thought of Queen Pinki. On the one hand, there was her behavior when they first met—her possibly attacking Thums-Up. Then there was the fact that she'd helped—or tried to help—them escape from Raja Rontu's soldiers not once but twice now. And then, of course, there was the fact that she'd helped get Raat and Snowy home to Sky Mountain when they were so sick.

"Queen Pinki's done a lot of bad things, but good things too," Kiya said finally.

"Word," agreed Kinjal. "Not at all like an evildoer in a story. Very multidimensional."

Kiya rolled her eyes at her brother. "And actually I have a confession to make, Princess . . ."

Kinjal cleared his throat. "Kiya, I don't think . . ."

Kiya shook her head and went on. "It was me who endangered Raat and Snowy. I asked them to fly down to see the wanted posters that Rontu's soldiers had put up. If I hadn't done that, they wouldn't have had to fly so fast or so hard. And then, when they were exhausted from flying, I forgot about the polluted waters . . ." Kiya's voice caught. "I was worried they were so tired and so I told them to drink from the poisonous river."

Princess Pakkhiraj was very quiet for a few moments, her eyes huge and searching. Kiya could feel the power of their force down to her soul. She fought to keep the tears down, but she couldn't, and they poured over her face. Kiya's chest heaved like it was splitting in two. Kinjal stood by her shoulder, but she could hardly feel his support. She kept her gaze fixed on the giant pakkhiraj horse. Would she forgive her? Could she?

Kiya felt her insides quake, like the very land under her feet was shifting.

19

A (Second) Plan Comes Together

FINALLY, AFTER A long moment when Kiya was sure Princess Pakkhiraj would kick her out of the Sky Kingdom altogether, the leader of the pakkhiraj horses smiled and said, "We are, none of us, perfect, are we?"

Kiya let out a strangled little sob. She could feel her hot cheeks still wet with tears. "No."

"But I trust in your good heart, as I know that Raat and Snowy do too," Princess Pakkhiraj added. "And the only thing we can do is to move forward and try to make sure no more pakkhiraj, or water pari, get sick again."

"How can we do that?" Kinjal asked, his worried eyes on Kiya's face.

Princess Pakkhiraj paced a bit back and forth, her wings

flapping in concentration while she thought. As she walked, she jingled the bells that were woven through her mane and dropped the flowers that grew through her hair like magic. "We cannot go to Raja Rontu to ask him to shut down the factories. Despite being your uncle, he is clearly not a fan of yours."

"He thinks we want his throne," Kiya explained with a sniffle.

"As if!" Kinjal scoffed. "I mean, I wouldn't mind having dudes serve me trays of sweets all day, but the rest of that royal stuff sounds like a major drag."

The princess stomped a heavy hoof, jingling some more. "Some people are so worried about keeping their power, they cannot see anything else."

"What I don't understand is that eventually people in his kingdom will start getting sick too," Kiya said. "It's not like they're immune from poison in the rain and water."

"They're too shortsighted to see that," said Princess Pakkhiraj.

"Sesha's clearly involved somehow too—but it's not like we can stroll into the Undersea Kingdom of Serpents and expect him to be happy about it," said Kiya. "And I don't think he'll volunteer to work with us to stop the acid rain."

"So what do we do?" Kinjal asked the princess. "I mean, for all we know, he's behind it!" He told the princess about the Great Blah and how even though they could no longer see it, they were pretty sure it had something to do with the poison in the waters.

"The Great Blah?" Princess Pakkhiraj's multicolored wings rose up like giant eyebrows. "Hmm, interesting. You say Sesha's favorite hench-monster is no longer manifesting in animate form but influencing emotions through these poisonous rains?"

The twins nodded in agreement.

"I wonder what Sesha did to it that the Great Blah decided to de-animate," mused the princess. "That horrible snake must have hurt its feelings for it to now decide to take over everyone else's emotions."

"It's weird when it happens, like someone's slowly crept into your mind and taken over your feelings." Kinjal shuddered, as if remembering the numbness that had come over him not once but twice now. "Making you feel like nothing you do matters. Like you can't make a difference anyway."

"That's called ennui," said Kiya in a *eureka* voice. "A feeling of sadness or dissatisfaction."

Kinjal rolled his eyes. "Okay, Dr. Encyclopedia."

Kiya just gave a harrumph. It was true that sometimes, when she was super bored, she liked to flip through their parents' ancient collection of encyclopedias. *Ennui* was one of the words she remembered, mostly because it was on the same page as a giant picture of an emu, which was one of her favorite Australian birds.

Princess Pakkhiraj smiled gently. "Knowledge is a more powerful weapon and a more potent magic than any other."

Her words made Kiya remember the power of yet another book—the *Thakurmar Jhuli* book of her father's. And it made her remember something else—a picture she had once seen in that collection of Bengali folktales. Quickly, she dug through her bag and brought out the ancient book, flipping to the page she remembered.

"I think I know where the Great Blah might be." Kiya pointed excitedly to the illustration on the page. "Look!"

A (SECOND) PLAN COMES TOGETHER

It was a picture of a doito—a big, hairy monster of Bengali folktales—sitting on the tippy top of a great mountain crying giant, poisonous tears that rained down on the villages below. And the way that the doito was illustrated, with great whorls of dirt and black clouds around it, made it look like it was at the center of a swirling, evil tornado.

"I remember that story!" Kinjal peered down at the page over her shoulder. "And the clouds around that monster definitely look like the Great Blah did when it kidnapped Thums-Up from our backyard the last time we came to this dimension!"

Princess Pakkhiraj nodded at them both. "I knew you two would find out what needs to be done."

The magic of Sky Mountain was so potent that it didn't take too long for Raat and Snowy to reemerge from the infirmary as healthy and strong as ever. Once again, their eyes were bright, their coats shiny, and their wings broad and powerful. Behind them danced out Thums-Up and Tuntuni. The dog-slash-pakkhiraj was still barking and jumping at the bird while the bird was telling an endless stream of jokes.

"What do you get when you cross a snail and a porcupine?" asked the bird. When Thums-Up didn't respond, he cackled, "A slowpoke!"

Thums-Up jumped up, flying around Tuni in a crooked circle even as the bird burbled, "Hey, doggy, why didn't the two fours stay for dinner?"

Thums-Up made a questioning sound, flying upside down with her ears flopping and tongue lolling out.

"Because they already ate!" Tuni whooped. "Get it? Ate? Eight?"

Thums-Up landed, whining and looking confused.

Raat and Snowy neighed, galloping toward the twins.

"You're better!" exclaimed Kinjal, running up to throw

one arm around each horse's neck. Of course, they were so tall, they had to bend a little to allow him to do so.

Thums-Up flew happily around her giant friends. She zipped and zoomed around them, now right side up, now upside down and sideways, her tongue lolling this way and that in her happiness.

Princess Pakkhiraj, along with Raat, Snowy, and Kinjal, laughed at Thums-Up's antics. "Someone seems very happy to see you both on your feet again," said the princess with a chuckle.

"Kiya?" said Raat, looking at her with a quizzical glance.

"Is everything all right?" asked Snowy, his voice full of concern.

Kiya glanced shyly at her friends. "I'm so sorry—it was my fault you got sick! My fault we even got chased by the soldiers in the first place!"

"Come here, friend," said Raat, and Kiya shuffled forward.

"Closer!" laughed Snowy, pulling Kiya toward them with a long wing. "It wasn't your fault!"

"You are always only trying your best, and that is what

we all must try to do," Princess Pakkhiraj agreed, her luminous eyes bright and supportive.

Kiya felt the love and trust of her friends lifting her up as if on wings, and felt her emotions healing with that magic, just as Raat's and Snowy's bodies had healed too.

"So I think we know what might be causing some of these poisonous rains." Kiya told her friends about all they had discussed, showing them the picture of the crying mountaintop doito from her father's folktale book.

20

The Mountains of Illusions

So THE BRILLIANT plan is we are supposed to go and give this horrible monster—the same one that tried to kidnap Thums-Up multiple times—a big hug?" asked Raat skeptically.

They were flying from Sky Mountain toward the Maya Pahar, which were also called the Maya Mountains, or the Mountains of Illusions. She wasn't sure, but Princess Pakkhiraj was guessing that was where they would find the Great Blah, on top of the highest mystical peak, crying.

"And how are we supposed to even get close to the monster?" Snowy flapped his wings hard against a wet current of air that lifted the horses slightly off track. "Remember, every time we go near it, it makes us all feel like nothing matters and we have no power to change anything anyway."

"Did that healing spell you guys got come with an extra helping of doubt or what?" cackled Tuni. Thums-Up, who'd apparently grown fond of the bird during their time together in the infirmary, was giving him a ride on her head. She yipped in agreement with her new friend.

Kiya didn't say anything out loud, but she was kind of surprised at her pakkhiraj friends being so doubt-y. Or were Raat and Snowy just questioning the plan because she had recently let them down so many times?

"Don't worry, guys," Kinjal assured the horses. "We talked to Princess Pakkhiraj, and she has a plan to help combat the way the Great Blah makes everyone numb."

"Hey, what do you call an elephant that doesn't matter?" Tuni burbled.

"Is this really relevant right now?" Kiya rolled her eyes toward the gray and as-always-drizzly sky. It had been raining for so long now, she hardly remembered what the sun felt like on her skin.

When everyone appeared to be ignoring Tuni's question,

Thums-Up's hackles rose and she growled as if protecting her friend.

In the end, it was Snowy who broke first. "I don't know, Tuntuni, what do you call an elephant that doesn't matter?" the horse asked.

"An irrelephant!" said the yellow bird triumphantly.

Thums-Up turned her head this way and that, as if confused. "I don't get it," said Kinjal.

"Neither do I," agreed Raat as he banked a little bit left to avoid a rain cloud.

"It's a joke based on the word *irrelevant*," Kiya explained, sighing with impatience at their joke-telling bird friend. "Get it? Irrelephant, irrelevant?"

"What's irrelevant?" Snowy snorted.

"Something that doesn't matter, doesn't count," said Kiya. Truth be told, she didn't only like to read through the encyclopedia when she was bored, but sometimes the dictionary too.

"Kind of like how the Great Blah makes us feel!" said Raat.

"But not after we put Princess Pakkhiraj's plan in action!" said Kinjal triumphantly.

THE MOUNTAINS OF ILLUSIONS

They had long left the top of Sky Mountain, and the Sky Kingdom. They had flown away from the great felled forests of the Kingdom Beyond with its newly sprung-up, smoke-spewing factories that dotted the landscape like squat, puffing, gray trolls. And now they were approaching the Maya Pahar—the Mountains of Illusions.

It was still raining, but the sky changed from a dull gray to a lighter gray streaked with pops of pink, blue, yellow, and purple. The clouds had become fluffy cotton puffs that bounced about, squeaking as if with personalities of their own. Everything was colorful and pastel, smelling vaguely sweet, like a dream or the inside of a candy shop, or both.

"This is Maya Pahar?" Kinjal asked, his voice full of awe. "It's like something out of a storybook!"

"Or from outer space!" Kiya peered around, wondering why everything she saw sparkled and shone like images of a distant galaxy she had seen sent from a powerful telescope.

"Well, over there is a birthplace of baby stars!" Snowy pointed a wing as both horses landed gently on a shifting landmass that giggled as if their hooves were tickling it.

"A star nursery?" Kiya had read about such a thing. "That's amazing! Can we go see?"

"I think we should concentrate on finding the Great Blah, don't you think?" her brother asked, and Kiya felt embarrassed she had let her scientific curiosity get the better of her logical, step-by-step mind.

"No, totally, you're totally right," she agreed quickly.

"Let's go that way, where the ground is rising!" Snowy suggested.

"Good idea," snorted Raat. "That should take us to the highest point of Maya Pahar!"

"We can't just fly up there?" asked Kiya, gazing up and up at the seemingly unending mountain.

"It's a pakkhiraj no-fly zone," explained Raat shortly, as if they should understand what that meant.

"Oh, sure, a no-fly zone," Kinjal agreed, shrugging at Kiya.

"And the last time Raat here broke a no-fly zone, there was some serious trouble." Snowy snickered at the memory. "All that paperwork—in triplicate!"

"Don't remind me," snapped Raat with a flash of teeth.

THE MOUNTAINS OF ILLUSIONS

As they walked uphill through the smushy, cloudlike land, Kiya saw that the trees around them were heavy with a kind of fruit that she had never seen before. The trunks were purple and the fruit a fuzzy pink.

"This place is amazing!" Kiya wished she had a camera to document what she was seeing, or some way to take samples of all the fascinating things around her.

Thums-Up chased one of the dancing pastel clouds, getting bopped in the nose by the cloud for her efforts. The dog-slash-pakkhiraj whined, putting her wings over her nose in surprise.

"Hey, what do you call a tree you can put in your hand?" asked Tuni as he flew from sparkly tree to sparkly tree, pecking absently at the fuzzy fruit.

"A hand-oak?" guessed Snowy.

"Arm candy!" shouted Kinjal.

"Neither of those answers makes any sense!" grumbled Raat as he carefully picked his way among the shifting clouds.

The ground was getting steep now, and the climbing up was all the harder for them, not being able to see where they were going. They were all stumbling and tripping on their own feet. And the pastel-colored clouds were darkening once again to grays and blacks, the atmosphere changing from bright to gloomy.

"The answer to your joke is a palm tree," said Kiya flatly, having heard the joke before at school.

Tuni made a disappointed *wah-wah* sound. "I wanted

to say the answer," he said in an aw-shucks kind of way, kicking a tiny cloud with a tiny foot.

"I don't think anyone else heard me," Kiya said by way of apology. She coughed, waving away some clouds from in front of her face. "Say it again."

Kinjal's entire head had become engulfed in a gray cloud. He waved and shook it away impatiently. "Yeah, I didn't hear the answer, Tuni!" he confirmed. "What do you call a tree you can put in your hand?"

"A palm tree!" the bird said with a triumphant trumpeting sound.

"Very clever!" said Raat, even as he almost tripped.

"Hilarious!" Snowy coughed as a cloud came along right in front of his face as he was talking. It was like the mountain itself didn't want them to get where they were going.

21

The Magic of Caring

IT WAS TREACHEROUS going to the top of Maya Pahar. The clouds made it impossible to see where they were walking and the ground beneath them seemed to give way at random times. The trees grew thick, blocking their way, and once in a while the fuzzy pink fruits fell, hitting them on the head when they least expected it. Worst of all, the clouds seemed to be laughing at them, giggling in silly high-pitched voices whenever one of them stumbled or fell.

"This is a weird place!" mumbled Kinjal. "Weirder than any story I've ever read."

"No kidding." Kiya pushed a branch out of her eyes, only to have it *boing* back and thwack her in the face again.

"What I wouldn't give for some of your warrior sloths right now."

Kinjal snorted with laughter, then coughed because a cloud was dancing around in front of his nose and mouth. "At least with their long arms they could keep some of these tree branches and clouds out of our way."

"Why are we heading up here anyway? It is such a long way," said Snowy suddenly, sounding grumpier than usual. The white horse stopped walking and seemed intent on turning around.

"We probably won't find that silly Blah creature anyway," Raat agreed, stopping next to his friend. He flicked his tail impatiently like he were chasing away flies. "Let's turn around."

Thums-Up barked, sharp and shrill. "You're right, girl!" Kiya exclaimed. "That's not you two talking—that's the influence of the Great Blah! We must be getting close! Time to institute the magic protection we've planned!"

"Hey, what d'ya call a dog who does magic?" burbled Tuntuni, who was back to hitching a ride on Thums-Up's back.

"You've told us this one before, Tuni," Kinjal said with a groaning laugh.

But the yellow bird ignored him. "You call him a labracadabrador!"

Thums-Up gave a shrill bark, shaking her head fiercely.

"Or her," Tuni agreed. "I stand corrected. You can call *her* a labracadabrador!"

"Hold up, everyone!" Kiya called, pulling out the trumpet-like ichha-chapa flower from her backpack. "I think it's time to protect ourselves from the Great Blah!"

"What are you going to do with that flower?" Raat asked with a snort that sounded like a harrumph.

"Nothing that will probably make any difference," sniffed Snowy. Neither horse had taken a step upward, but they hadn't turned around either.

"This *will* make a difference," said Kiya patiently. "We planned out this magical protection with Princess Pakkhiraj."

"The reason we're all starting to feel numb, like nothing matters, is because we're getting close to the Great Blah,"

Kinjal explained. "I'm feeling it too. It just feels hopeless and useless to even try. Like who cares anyway."

"But how can we stop from feeling this way?" Raat asked through a huge yawn. "Everything just feels silly and pointless."

"Goofy and useless," added Tuntuni, scratching his yellow head.

"Dull and irrelevant," snorted Snowy.

"Ridiculous and meaningless," said Kinjal with a sigh.

"Almost everyone who meets the Great Blah feels this way," said Kiya. "Except the water pari. There's something about their magic that protects them from that feeling that nothing matters, that sense of ennui." Kiya beamed, proud that she'd been able to use her new vocabulary word in a sentence, but no one seemed to have registered. She sighed. What was the point, after all?

"Let's just turn around and go home, eh?" Raat snorted.

"Back to Sky Mountain," agreed Snowy, laying back his ears.

"Back to Queen Pinki and the palace," corrected Tuni.

"Back home to New Jersey and our warm beds," yawned Kinjal.

Thums-Up barked and wagged her tail, like she was thinking of her cozy doggy bed in Parsippany, New Jersey, too.

"Stop! Hang in there, everyone! We still have a mission to accomplish!" Kiya urged, blowing into the trumpetlike flower with all her might.

And as the magic from the flower swirled all around them, they each grew still and quiet. The colors of Princess Pakkhiraj's magic flower were different from the naughty pastel clouds of Maya Pahar, which laughed at them as they tripped. This magic was vibrant, rich colors of healing and love that wrapped around and around each of them like the comforting end of a mother's silken sari. The magic tucked itself around them, cradling them, transforming them into a shape that was immune from the numbing spell of the Great Blah.

"Wait a minute! You have scales!" Snowy's eyes widened as he took in Raat's new, magicked form.

"You have them too! And gills!" Raat neighed, staring

back at Snowy. "What have you done to us, Kiya?"

"You have fins!" Tuntuni pointed at Thums-Up. The tiny bird's eyes were round like saucers.

Thums-Up barked at her new birdie friend. "She says you have them too!" Kiya translated.

"And sparkly tails!" Kinjal said, looking down at his sister's now disappeared legs.

"This time, you have one too!" Kiya told him, raising one eyebrow.

And it was true: They were all transformed by the magic of Princess Pakkhiraj's flower into strange half-mermaid shapes. Raat, Snowy, and Thums-Up still had their own wings and front legs, but scaly tails and fins. Kiya and Kinjal had both transformed into water pari, while Tuntuni looked the funniest of all, with his birdie top and wings and tiny yellow water-pari tail.

"When we figured out that the mermaid magic protected them from the Great Blah, we knew it was a way to protect us from losing our direction and nerve, our purpose up here on the Maya Mountains," Kiya explained.

"But we have no legs," squawked Tuni.

"Or only two," said Snowy, mournfully indicating his front legs and back mer-horse tail.

"How are we supposed to make it the rest of the way up the mountain?" Raat asked. "It's too dangerous to fly with all this cloud cover, and none of us can walk properly anymore."

"True!" agreed Kiya. "But we can swim through the clouds!" She couldn't believe her attitude toward being a mermaid had changed so much in such a short time.

"I can't swim!" Tuni burbled. "I'm a bird! I belong in the sky!"

"Don't worry! The princess put some extra-special magic in that flower so we could swim through these clouds on Maya Pahar!" said Kinjal. He had obviously been able to brush off the feeling of not caring, and was grinning at all his friends now. "Ready, everyone?"

"Ready?" squawked Tuntuni. "Ready for what?"

The three pakkhiraj looked equally skeptical.

"Ready to swim to the top of the mountain!" announced Kinjal. He closed his eyes and held out his hands, as if about to do a breaststroke, but nothing happened.

"Hate to tell you, but nothing's happening, champ," burbled Tuntuni.

"Are we to be in this ungraceful form forever?" asked Raat mournfully.

"What will the other pakkhiraj say?" squawked Snowy. "Flying horses with sparkling tails! The humiliation!"

"Calm down, it's only temporary." Kiya reassuringly patted them both. "I didn't like being a mermaid either at first. But I've come to realize there's a time and a place for magic."

"Huh, Dr. Perfecto believing in magic over science! That's what they call character growth in a story!" Kinjal opened his eyes temporarily to say.

"Keep concentrating, bro!" Kiya said sternly. "And I didn't say I believed in magic more than science, just that each has its time and place."

"Aye, aye, captain!" And with a grin, Kinjal closed his eyes again, and this time, he slowly began swimming through the low-lying clouds on the mountain.

"You did it!" Kiya cheered. "You're swimming through the clouds!" Imitating her brother, she started making a swimming motion too. It took a minute to get the hang of it, but when she did, Kiya found that swimming through the clouds was almost as easy as swimming through water.

"It worked! The plan worked!" Kinjal enthused.

"Thank goodness!" Kiya agreed.

"We're swimming to the top of the mountain?" asked Snowy, looking around in astonishment. On Kinjal's instruction, both horses were wiggling their tails and slowly moving through the clouds as if through water.

"We're swimming to the top of the mountain!" cheered Raat as Thums-Up yipped happily, doing a few backward mid-cloud somersaults.

Only Tuni still seemed skeptical. "Birds are supposed to fly!"

Kiya ignored the complaining bird. "Well, at least now we're all protected from the magic of the Great Blah! The water pari's magic is that they all care so much—and now they've shared that with us!"

"We don't *not* care anymore, right?" Kinjal asked.

Raat and Snowy whinnied, kicking up their front legs through the clouds. "We care!"

Thums-Up barked in agreement.

"We care!" agreed Kiya.

And then they all looked at Tuntuni, who was looking mournfully at his yellow tail, experimentally flicking it this way and that. When he felt all their eyes on him, he let out a great sigh. "We care a lot," he agreed.

"So let's go find this monster!" said Kinjal with determination, as they all swam on.

22

Monsters Have Feelings Too

THE GREAT BLAH was sitting, as they had guessed, on the very top of the Maya Mountains. It was hard to see its form, as cloaked as it was in swirling, whirling clouds of black and gray. But, from their hiding place behind one of the colorful clouds, they managed to get a good look at it. Like in the illustration from their baba's copy of *Thakurmar Jhuli*, the monster did have a form within that cloudy tornado. It was a hairy, strong-limbed doito, dirty-faced and long-fanged, its filthy talons crooked and unkempt, its toenails so long they were curling in on themselves.

"Nasty!" Kinjal wrinkled his nose.

"Someone needs a pedicure!" singsonged Tuntuni. "And maybe a manicure too!"

Thums-Up, who'd had the most direct contact with the monster, being almost kidnapped by it not once but twice, gave out a low snarl, showing her teeth and raising her hackles.

"Shush, you three!" Kiya gave Thums-Up a reassuring pet to calm her down. The poor thing stopped growling, but her body stayed on high alert, her fur spiky at her back.

"Now that we've made it here, what do we do?" Kinjal asked.

"We do what all good scientists do," Kiya said.

"Clean a bunch of beakers?" asked Kinjal. "Get excited about Bunsen burners? Use long words that no one understands?"

"No, we stay quiet and observe him!" Kiya frowned ferociously at her brother, feeling a bit like a doito herself.

And so, observe him they did. The strange thing was, rather than doing regular monster things—like kidnapping innocent pets, or ransacking villages, or uprooting trees and knocking down buildings—the monster was crying. Like serious, boo-hoo crying that was so loud, it probably made it impossible for him to hear their approach. Then for a while he snuffled, crying lonely tears that dripped off his chin, leaving streak marks through the dirt on his face. Then, for a longer while, he bawled, sobbing, shaking tears that rained down on the ground below like a torrent of raindrops.

"He's making the acid rain?" asked Snowy.

"I think so," agreed Kiya, pointing to some pollution that was swirling up from the ground below. With every breath, the doito breathed in the gray-black clouds, and then his tears fell out in the same color. "I think he's transforming the factory pollution into polluted rain!"

"How do we find out why?" asked Tuni. "How do we make him stop?"

"What do you do when anyone is sad?" Kinjal asked simply. "You go up to them, sit by them, and ask them."

"No, wait, Kinjal, I think we should observe him more." Kiya tried to hold him back, but her brother, who had always been kind to people who were hurting, swam bravely forward.

The Great Blah looked up in surprise to have a water pari come sit on the ledge next to him, but not enough surprised to stop crying.

"I'm sorry you're so sad," offered Kinjal simply. He awkwardly settled his mer-tail so he was sitting with his legs dangling off a cloud.

The doito stared at Kinjal for a moment before pulling a giant snot-dangle up into his nose, then rubbing his forearm across his still drippy nostrils. "What do you care? What does anyone care?" His voice was deep, and scratchy like sandpaper.

That's when Kiya swam forward too, sitting with her tail folded under her on the other side of the Great Blah. "We care. We care about all the creatures of this land."

The Great Blah let out a hiccup of distress. "It doesn't matter, all that caring. It doesn't help anything, doesn't do anything, you know."

"Maybe not." It was Raat, swimming over now too.

"But if it can help, isn't it worth trying?" Now it was Snowy, who had come over with a nervous-looking Thums-Up beside him. Kiya felt very proud of her pet for having the courage to come forward despite her fears.

The final member of the group to join them was Tuntuni. "Hey, G.B.," burbled the bird in a funny, comedian-like voice. "I know you go by the Great Blah, but can I call you G.B.? It seems more friendly-like."

The monster gave a confused shrug, batting a cloud away with a clawed, hairy hand. "I guess."

"Wonderful! Wonderful!" said Tuni, puffing out his little yellow chest. "So did you hear the one about Albert Einstein's brother Frank?"

The doito scratched with long talons at his greasy hair, breaking off a few giant flakes of dandruff that floated from the mountain down to the ground below. Kiya wondered if there was someone who was about to get a very gross and strangely snowy surprise down there.

"No, what about Albert Einstein's brother?" the monster finally mumbled through his tears.

"I mean, Albert was a genius, but his brother Frank? He was a monster!" laughed Tuni.

"Hey, that's mean!" said the doito, his eyes flashing and a torrent of mist swirling around him. He pounded one giant fist down onto the mountain, sending a shower of stones tumbling down. "Are you saying I'm a monster?"

"No! It's a joke!" said Tuni quickly, backing up a little.

"If his last name is Einstein, then his name is Frank Einstein—get it?" asked Kinjal encouragingly.

Raat, Snowy, and Thums-Up exchanged worried looks.

"Which sounds like Frankenstein—who is a storybook monster in our dimension," Kiya added hurriedly. No one wanted to see the Great Blah go from crying to furious just now. "With green skin and bolts coming out of his neck."

"Bolts?" squawked Tuni. "That can't be comfortable."

"I don't suppose it is." Kinjal turned to Kiya. "Hey, do you think Ma would buy me a Frankenstein costume this year for Halloween?"

"Not the time," Kiya said with a warning look.

Suddenly, the Great Blah stood up with a terrible yell, stretching up toward the heavens. Thums-Up gave a startled growl, diving for cover behind Raat and Snowy, who put out their wings and stamped their front feet as if preparing for battle. Unfortunately, their back legs were still in the shape of water-pari tails, so this wasn't particularly intimidating. Tuni gave a squawk and dived under Kiya's armpit, from where she had a heck of a time fishing the little bird out.

Kinjal, for his part, put out his hands and said things like "Whoa there, easy now," as if trying to calm an upset horse.

"Maybe this wasn't the best plan," Kiya whispered to Kinjal.

"You don't say?" he shot back.

23

Jokes Are Good Medicine

THAT'S WHEN SOMETHING surprising happened.

"Tell me more jokes," demanded the Great Blah, baring his bright yellow teeth. "Funny jokes! I want to laugh."

Now everyone exchanged worried looks. "Funny jokes, funny jokes." Kinjal tapped on the side of his temple as if trying to reboot his mental computer.

When no one spoke for a moment, the monster roared, a noise that made them all jump, Tuni turning head over tail in flight. The doito's boogery nostrils were flared and crooked teeth bared. "Want more funny jokes NOW!"

"It's hard to be funny under duress!" protested Snowy, and Thums-Up whined in agreement, flapping her rainbow-colored wings as if unsure whether to fly away.

"Funny words!" the doito yelled, this time even louder. The very clouds seemed to reverberate with the force of his yells. "Now!"

They all looked, alarmed, at each other. Someone had to come up with a good joke, and pronto!

"Um, okay, okay, I've got one!" Kiya burbled. She licked her lips nervously. Her heart was hammering in her chest so loud her ears rang from it.

Kinjal grimaced at her. "Sis, I love you, I do. But I'm sorry, you're really not known for your sense of humor . . ." he said in a low voice, his eyes on the monster the whole time.

Kiya made dagger eyes at him and he backed off. "Okay, okay, I was just saying," he muttered.

"What is joke! Tell me the joke!" shouted the Great Blah, scattering tears off his face and down the mountain. His arms were whirling around him, which made the swirling clouds whirl around him too, giving him the appearance of a tornado again.

"He's going to bring the entire mountain down!" shouted Raat, his mane flying wildly.

"Hurry! Tell the joke!" yelled Snowy. "Any joke!"

"Here it is! Here's the joke!" Kiya put out her hands in a protective gesture even as her braids got lifted off her back from the force of his wind.

"Tell him!" urged Tuni, who was trying to keep from flying away by gripping on to Thums-Up's collar. "Before this guy gives us all a good reason to cry!"

"Um, okay, okay." Kiya licked her dry lips again as the Great Blah continued to whirl and rage. Luckily, the mermaid magic was keeping them from feeling that sense of numbness and ennui, but it wouldn't protect them from being blown away by the force of the monster's storm.

"Hurry up already!" Kinjal urged as he hung on to Raat to keep steady.

"Yes, please!" Raat agreed, his wings now flying up from the Great Blah's rising storm.

"Why do bees always have sticky hair?" shouted Kiya over the noise of the whirling winds.

When the Great Blah didn't react at all, she gave her brother a confused look.

"He didn't hear you over that storm he's whipping up!" Kinjal shouted. "Here, let's ask together!"

And together, on three, they shouted, "Why do bees always have sticky hair?"

But the monster still hadn't heard the question, swirling faster and faster in his tornado dance. Soon they would all be carried away by the force of the stormy winds.

"All of us! Let's all of us ask together!" yelled Kiya.

And so, the twins, the horses, and Tuni all shouted at the tops of their lungs, "Why do bees always have sticky hair?"

Finally, the monster seemed to have heard their question. He slowed down his spinning, becoming less of a tornado and more of a visible doito again. "Is this a joke?" he asked slowly, huffing through his yellow teeth.

"Yes! A joke!" agreed Kinjal.

"A funny joke!" shouted Tuni.

"Don't get his hopes up too much!" muttered Kiya. "It's not all *that* funny."

"Well, you've got to finish what you started now!" urged Raat.

"Tell him the punch line!" said Snowy.

The doito sat back down on the cliffside with a heavy thump. "I don't know the answer! I never know the answer!

Why don't I ever know the answer to anything?" He started weeping again, boo-hooing loudly and forcefully, sending another shower of acid rain from his eyes to the ground below.

"Don't worry! I don't know the answer to a lot of things!" said Kiya honestly. "And I get upset about it sometimes too, but it's okay! It's okay not to know but to be willing to learn!"

Kinjal shot her a knowing smile. "So tell him why bees always have sticky hair, and then next time, G.B. will be able to tell the joke to someone else."

"Like Sesha! I'll tell Sesha!" enthused the monster as everyone else tried to keep their reactions to themselves.

"Bees have sticky hair because they use honeycombs!" Kiya said with a laugh.

The doito looked blank. Worse, like it might begin its tornado-ing again.

"Hang on to your tails, friends," muttered Snowy.

Raat moaned softly, shaking his head. "There is nothing in the pakkhiraj handbook about this. I was not trained for this."

"Get it? Honeycombs—like hair combs made of honey?" prompted Kinjal. "*Honey*combs?"

The Great Blah's face was blank, and then, as understanding washed over him, it sharpened into focus. "Honeycombs, because if you had honey on your comb it would make your hair sticky!" He ran his dirty fingers through his already matted hair, imitating the gesture of a comb.

"Exactly!" Kiya clapped her hands for the doito, and Kinjal joined. Their animal friends neighed, barked, and tweeted in appreciation.

"I like your joke. It's funny!" The Great Blah stood and cheered, clapping alongside everyone else.

When everyone quieted down, Kinjal studied the Great Blah's face. "So why were you so sad in the first place?"

The doito stopped smiling right away and sat down with a great thump. Kiya was pretty sure she heard the cloud he landed on squeak in pain. "I thought Sesha was my friend."

"But then you slowly discovered your best friend was a homicidal maniac who thrives on violence?" Tuntuni said sympathetically. "I hate it when that happens."

"That didn't really bother me." The Great Blah scratched absently at an open, oozing boil on his arm.

"You realized he's just in it for the power and glory?" suggested Snowy.

"I liked that about Sesha, actually." The Great Blah gave a little grin of happiness, making everyone else roll their eyes. "It's kind of cute."

"You saw how his actions were hurting the kingdom?" Raat neighed.

"Are they?" The Great Blah picked at his nose with a blank expression.

"Then what is it?" Kiya asked impatiently. "What's the problem?"

"Sesha didn't . . . he didn't . . ." The monster started crying once again, big fat tears that fell wetly off his filthy face. "He didn't come to my birthday paaaaaaaarty!" he wailed.

24

A Birthday Fit for a Monster

"YOU'RE KIND OF selfish, you know that?" Kiya scolded the doito. "If you were really Sesha's friend, you would tell him honestly how much he's hurting the kingdom."

"What if I don't wanna?" whined the monster, sticking a giant finger up his drippy nose.

"Doing the right thing isn't always the same as doing the easy thing," Kiya said primly.

"Hey, are you forgetting something?" hissed Kinjal.

"What?" Kiya muttered back, her braids whipping over her shoulder as she turned to look at her brother.

"That this is a monster that could seriously hurt us?" Kinjal whisper-yelled.

"Right, so maybe cool it with the mom lectures?" Tuntuni squawked, hopping from Thums-Up's shoulder to Kinjal's.

But the doito looked shamefacedly at Kiya. "Why's Sesha hurting the kingdom?" he asked, digging industriously into a wet nostril with a long nail.

"Don't you know the damage all this acid rain is having on the creatures below?" Kiya asked. "Before you have any sort of party, I'm going to need you to understand what you've done!"

"Along with the factory pollution, et cetera!" Kinjal added helpfully.

"Yes, absolutely," agreed Kiya.

And that's how they all decided to return to the shores of Pari-desh. They had to de-mermaid themselves first, which involved getting the Great Blah to promise not to change any of their feelings.

"If we start not to care, we won't care about your birthday either," said Kiya sternly, and the rest of them nodded in agreement.

"Okay, okay, I won't tornado your feelings," said the

Great Blah in his gritty voice. "I promise."

And so, with another bugle-blow into the ichha-chapa flower, Kiya magicked away the mermaid tails and fins she and her friends had developed. The horses stomped all four of their feet in appreciation. Thums-Up did dive bomb after dive bomb on the fluffy clouds, rolling happily on her back with all four feet in the air. Tuni whistled and sang, swirling around their heads, while Kinjal gave Kiya a grateful look.

"I've never been so happy to have legs!" he said, patting down his jeans.

"Same!" Kiya agreed.

After making their way down the mountain, they took the doito to the edge of the Pari-desh ocean. The stink of rotten fish was even worse than before, and the piles of dead sea creatures even higher.

"Why are all these fishes so dead?" the monster asked, wrinkling his nose.

"It's because of your acid rain!" Kiya explained, not sure she understood the entire science and magic of what was

happening, but okay for now to just accept that she didn't know and still try to do her best for her new friends.

"Your tears are hurting the fish and the other sea creatures," Kinjal said. "Including the water pari, who care for all the others who live under the sea."

"There's no such thing as water pari!" scoffed the doito as he scratched his armpit. "They're just in stories!"

"We're going to take you to meet them now!" said Kiya, holding out her hand to the doito. "And anyway, someone could say the same about you!"

Snowy and Raat had sent a magical message ahead of their arrival, so Shonali and the other water pari were waiting for them, bobbing at the surface of the polluted waters for their signal. The sea was still covered in foam and there was still brown sludgy stuff in the water. But now that the doito had stopped crying, the rains had actually stopped and the sun was out, lighting up the surface of the water and dancing off the waves. The water pari swam toward the group of friends, perching up on the jutting rocks where they had once sunned themselves.

"You see? Water pari aren't just in stories!" Kiya pointed at the mermaids.

"And even if you learn about something in a story, that doesn't mean it's not true," added Kinjal.

"I hope they sing," sighed Snowy. "I love water pari song!"

"I hate the water," mumbled Raat, giving the water pari a cautious look.

Shonali, in the meantime, had come the farthest forward, peering at the doito's face. He stared back at her, a little mesmerized by her kind expression.

"We hear that you had a birthday, but no one came to your party?" Shonali asked the doito. Her tone was gentle, her voice like a song.

"I was very sad," said the Great Blah with a huge sigh. He sat down heavily on the sandy shore.

"I can imagine," said another of the water pari kindly, leaning over from her perch on a rock. "It's normal to be sad sometimes."

"But you can't be sad all the time!" burbled a little mermaid with a pink sparkly tail and wings.

"Which is why we've decided to throw you a belated birthday party now," Shonali announced as all her fellow water pari cheered.

"A birthday party?" The Great Blah looked absolutely shocked, his eyes wide and smile delighted. He scratched his head with long nails as if this would help him understand what was going on. "Really? You would do that? For me?"

"We water pari care about all creatures," Shonali reassured him with a smile. "It's who we are."

"Plus it's always a good time for a mermaid-themed birthday party!" announced Kinjal with a grin at his sister.

Kiya laughed, nodding. "It's always a good time for a magical birthday party!"

So with a clapping of Mermaid Prime Minister Shonali's hands, there arrived a line of lobsters carrying seaweed garlands for everyone's necks, and a giant crab carrying a coral crown for the birthday doito's head. There were seaside games and delicious honey-and-nectar cakes, courtesy of the bees that Kiya and Kinjal had saved on their last visit.

There was, of course, the beautiful music of the water pari's singing, as well as the slightly less melodious barking of Thums-Up. The horses, twins, and even the doito danced about at the shoreline to the music of the mermaids. With the doito no longer creating acid rain with his endless tears, there was less of the foamy pollution on the water, and as they all played among the waves, the water no longer stung their skin. There was even less of the red-brown pollution visible.

It wasn't gone, but the water and sky were definitely clearing up.

The birthday party was a huge success, despite how different everyone was from each other. There were games that lasted into the night, including pin the tail on the seagull and go fish with waterproof cards. Some playful dolphins decided to join them at the shoreline, leaping into the air and doing flips, all the while gossiping with the mermaids in their screeching language. Tuntuni told a series of horrible, silly jokes and the entire group laughed at each and every one. Raat and Snowy gave the water pari gentle horseback rides on the beach, with the mermaids sitting sidesaddle, whooping with joy as they galloped over the sand. Raat still wasn't willing to wade in and get wet, but you can't have everything.

The Great Blah's face wasn't sad anymore but bright and laughing. His dark, stormy coat had disappeared—the swirling tornado he had once always worn to disguise his true self and true feelings. He still wasn't Kiya's favorite monster, but now that he was coming out of his destructive and uncaring shell, he was growing on her.

Kinjal spent some time teaching the doito to skip stones at the shoreline, and the mermaids invited him to add his voice to their songs. They even saw some live—and healthy-looking—flying fish leaping out of the waves, as if dancing to the water-pari music.

"We may be one, we may feel small," Shonali and her friends sang. "But even one can be mighty and tall! To care, to try, to feel, to cry—these change us from one alone to us all!"

There were still many problems to fix, but for now, they were enjoying themselves with their new friends—eating, singing, playing, and dancing. Kiya remembered how Princess Pakkhiraj had told her that joy and laughter were a necessary part of making change, and Kiya thought she was beginning to understand.

"Everything is connected to everything," she sang softly to herself.

At first, it was only her brother who joined her, but then each of their friends heard and joined in her song.

"Everything is connected to everything," they sang, clapping in rhythm to the words. "But how?"

The answer, of course, was love. Everything was connected to everything by love. In their own and every other galaxy, every other version of the universe. Throughout space and time, through sadness and joy, through it all, everything was connected to everything.

By love.

25

A Close Encounter of the Snaky Kind

THEY HADN'T SOLVED all the problems of the Sky Kingdom or the Kingdom Beyond, but they had made the sun come out again. Even though Rontu's factories were still producing pollution, and therefore some acid rain, the skies above them had finally cleared up, inviting in the light, now that the Great Blah had stopped crying.

"We can take you back to the Mountains of Illusions, if that's where you would like to go," offered Raat.

But the Great Blah refused. "I'm going to stay here, protecting the shore for the water pari and keeping an eye out for those nasty eels! The pari promised they'll teach me more songs when they come up to sun themselves," he explained.

A CLOSE ENCOUNTER OF THE SNAKY KIND

"Instead of being an evil hench-monster," said Shonali warmly, "I've suggested he might take up a career in singing!"

Kiya and Kinjal exchanged wide-eyed glances. To say the doito had a terrible voice was being generous, but who were they to judge?

"I'm going to stay here awhile too," said Tuntuni. "And teach our new friend G.B. here a few more jokes!"

"Funny jokes! Funny jokes!" cheered the doito, and Kiya wondered if the yellow bird hadn't found the perfect audience for his enormous collection of ridiculous riddles.

And then it was time for the rest of them to head home. They said goodbye fondly to Shonali and the rest of the water pari, to Tuntuni and the Great Blah, who wasn't so blah-y anymore. The merry group cheered and waved them off from the shoreline.

They had only been flying for a short amount of time, though, when all three pakkhiraj started acting agitated. First it was Thums-Up, flying in awkward, upside-down zigzags. But their dog-slash-pakkhiraj-horse wasn't the best flier anyway, so Kiya didn't pay attention to that at first. When Snowy and Raat started flying slower and slower, however, Kiya knew something was up.

"What's the matter?" she asked, but before the horses could answer, her brother looked over at her from Raat's back.

"Something's not right, I can feel it. Like that feeling I get in a haunted house." Kinjal rubbed at his arms.

"You just have goose bumps," Kiya began saying, but then she got that creepy feeling too. "Someone's coming!" she said, not sure at all how she knew that.

Raat and Snowy immediately began looking this way and that, on high alert.

"We've got to find somewhere to hide!" Kinjal said, not sure how he knew that.

"Behind this rain cloud!" Raat and Snowy flew to their midair hiding spot, Thums-Up barely making it in time before he arrived.

It was Sesha, the horrifyingly evil King of the Serpents, riding through the air in his green, glowing chariot. His green velvet cloak streamed out behind him, and giant jeweled rings flashed on every finger. His green-black eyes flashed like lightning and his shiny hair was coiled and slicked back as if with rain.

"Ride, my storm snakes, ride!" he called out, pointing forward into the sky. "Now that I've lost the Great Blah, that fool of a doito, I'm going to need you snakes to help me make chaos down below!"

And that's when they saw who Sesha had trailing behind him. Serpents in the shape of storms—making rain, hail, and thunder in their wake. They covered up the light of the sun, so that the early morning felt again like night.

"It's the serpent storm surge the eels were talking about!" whispered Kinjal.

"But so many more of them!" Kiya felt her heart hammering in her chest at the sight of the evil Serpent King with so many flying hench-snakes behind him.

Kiya and Kinjal, along with their pakkhiraj friends, huddled together behind the cloud. The horses kept their position by slowly flapping their wings—something like treading water but in midair.

"He'll kill us if he sees us," Kiya muttered, and Thums-Up softly whined.

"Don't forget, we have powers too," her brother reminded her. "And two of the best fighters in all the Sky Kingdom." He nodded toward Raat and Snowy, who had, on their last encounter with Sesha, fought with a fierceness and bravery that was breathtaking.

"What is he doing? Why is he calling forth so many storms?" whispered Raat.

Snowy shook his head, equally perplexed. "There are too many of them to fight!"

"Where is my tornado wind?" asked Sesha, his sharp

teeth glinting in the fading sunlight. He reached out and dragged a giant green-black serpent around him like a second cloak, whirling in the center of a fierce and violent storm.

"Now for some floods!" shouted Sesha, ordering a rain-cloud-wielding serpent to create such torrential rains that the ground below them seemed to fall away.

"He's making a mudslide down below!" Kiya whispered, her eyes huge.

Kinjal pointed down to the villages of the Kingdom Beyond. "Those houses are sliding away! That mud's like lava!"

And then, to their utter horror and amazement, Sesha flashed a lightning rod of green fire from his hand, straight down from the sky to the ground! Wherever the lightning struck, there bloomed a wildfire! The fire was like a hungry, speeding snake, slithering across the land, eating the houses, trees, and anything else in its path.

Sesha laughed as he looked down on the destruction he was wreaking below, looking every bit like a villain from one of the fantasy stories Kinjal loved so much. It was only when the green chariot and its accompanying storm snakes rode away, in response to the bellowed command of "Forward! To more destruction!" that they all felt like they could let out a breath.

"We have to go down and help those people!" Kiya urged.

"Between the rains and floods, the fires and mudslides, it's a complete disaster down there!" Kinjal cried in alarm. "There are going to be so many people in danger!"

"That seems to be Sesha's goal," said Raat grimly.

"Destruction for destruction's sake, that is the worst kind of evil!" Snowy sounded like he was going to cry.

The friends landed down on the devastated ground in the Kingdom Beyond. Raat and Snowy transported families who were stuck on their roofs from the rising floodwaters. Thums-Up calmed down frightened children, licking away their tears. Raising his arms above his head—not unlike how Sesha had done it, but with a totally different goal in mind—Kinjal made rain clouds appear over the areas where the Serpent King's hench-snakes had lit forest fires. The rains he conjured weren't the torrents that the serpent storm surge had made. Rather, Kinjal's rains gently put out the flames, stopping the fires from spreading and creating any more damage than they already had.

"You've got to try to stop those mudslides!" Kinjal urged Kiya. "I can't! If I add any more water to them, it'll only make it worse!"

"I don't know if I can!" Kiya stared with huge eyes at the disastrous mud sliding down the mountains, devastating the houses and nature in its path.

"You can! You have crazy powerful magic!" Kinjal urged. "I believe in you!"

"All right! I'll try!" Kiya cried, putting her hands to the ground. She closed her eyes, nervous, as always, to trust what was more magic than science.

But with a touch of her hands to the land, Kiya felt her power surge. She felt the steady, rooted nature of her magic connecting her to the ground below, to everything good and green that grew upward from the soil to the sky. Kiya felt herself connect to this power that had always been inside her, feeling it shoot up her spine and through her limbs like she herself was a tree rising from deep roots and stretching toward the sun.

THE POISON WAVES

"The land is to grow things, not to harm them!" she whispered.

And with her touch, Kiya opened up the ground below her feet, making it suck in the excess floodwaters and dry the destructive mudslides.

"Good job!" Kinjal cheered. "You did it!"

Kiya felt exhausted, but proud too. Then she looked around. They had helped stop more destruction from happening, but they hadn't reversed the damage that Sesha and his serpent storm surge had already caused. Kiya felt even more tired, her head throbbing in an ache of sorrow at all the meaningless loss, all the pointless chaos.

Even though the Great Blah was gone, Kiya felt a hopelessness shoot through her, threatening to fell her like lightning toppling even the strongest of trees. "If Sesha keeps running around with those storm snakes, making floods and tornadoes and fires, this land will keep going through this!" she said sadly.

"Then we'll have to return!" Kinjal said, gripping her hand. "If they don't stop, we don't stop either!"

Kiya met her brother's eyes, and felt his magic, energetic and wild. Like two hands joining, she reached out her own steady, grounded magic to meet his. Their magics were like two sides of the same coin, she realized, balancing each other's energies, making each other better always.

She reached out her magic, drawing Raat, Snowy, and Thums-Up into their circle of power.

"We won't stop caring," Raat reassured her, drawing his dark wings around them all.

"We won't stop working to make things better," Snowy added with a dazzling horsey grin.

"We won't stop trying our hardest," Kinjal promised, and Thums-Up barked in loving agreement.

Kiya felt the power of her friends and family all around her. Perhaps each of them wasn't strong enough to halt all this destruction of the land and waters, air and nature, but together, they had a serious chance.

"We won't stop," Kiya repeated firmly. "Not until we find a way to stop Sesha!"

✦ AUTHOR'S NOTE ✦

The Poison Waves is the second novel in the Secrets of the Sky series, and like the previous book, *The Chaos Monster*, it is set in the same Kingdom Beyond multiverse of the three Kiranmala and the Kingdom Beyond books (*The Serpent's Secret, Game of Stars*, and *The Chaos Curse*) and the two Fire Queen books (*Force of Fire* and *Crown of Flames*). Brother and sister twins Kinjal and Kiya of the Secrets of the Sky series even live in the same town as Kiranmala— Parsippany, New Jersey—although their story probably takes place a few years before Kiranmala's begins.

Like the other Kingdom Beyond novels, *The Poison Waves* draws from many traditional Bengali folktales and children's stories. These are stories beloved in West Bengal (India), Bangladesh, and throughout the Bengali-speaking diaspora.

Thakurmar Jhuli and Pakkhiraj Horses
In 1907, Dakshinaranjan Mitra Majumdar published some classic Bengali folktales in a book called *Thakurmar Jhuli*

(Grandmother's Satchel). My parents and grandparents read to me often from an old, tattered, silver-covered copy of this book of folktales. Hearing these stories connected me to my heritage, lighting my imagination on fire with tales about princes and princesses from the Kingdom Beyond Seven Oceans and Thirteen Rivers, as well as stories about evil serpent kings, soul-stealing bhoot, and rhyming, carnivorous rakkhosh. I was so inspired by this book of folktales, I wrote my multiple middle grade series reimagining these old stories. That's why Kiya and Kinjal's copy of *Thakurmar Jhuli* appears in this story as a powerful, magical object—something all books can be!

Pakkhiraj horses—or winged, flying horses—are a huge part of the *Thakurmar Jhuli* stories: Princes and princesses are always flying off on adventures on pakkhiraj-back. Raat/Midnight and Snowy/Tushar Kona are the same flying horses who appear in the Kiranmala series as well as the Fire Queen books. In my mind, these are horses who might not be immortal, but have a very long life-span. Although there are no horses who disguise themselves as family dogs in the original *Thakurmar Jhuli* stories, I loved the idea of a family pet with a secret life and magical powers. Thums-Up is named after my favorite Indian cola brand, which I would enjoy every time I visited my extended family!

Bengali Mermaids

Bengali mermaids, or jol pari, are a kind of fairy that lives in the water. So Bengali mermaids don't just have fins and tails, but wings as well. They appear in folk- and fairy tales, and often wield powerful magic. While they're not as common or popular as some other kinds of magical creatures in regional folklore, Bengali water pari—like African and Caribbean mermaids—prove that mermaids exist in many cultures around the world!

Rakkhosh Stories

Folktales involving rakkhosh are very popular throughout South Asia. The word is sometimes spelled *rakshasa* in other parts of the region, but in this book, it is spelled like the word sounds in Bengali. Folktales are an oral tradition, passed on from one generation to the next, with each teller adding nuance to their own version.

Indrani, the twins' mother, is revealed to be a rakkhoshi, but she doesn't appear in either *Thakurmar Jhuli* or the other Kingdom Beyond books—although I imagine she is one of the revolutionaries who works with Arko and Chandni in *Crown of Flames*. Arko, the twins' father, appears in the other Kingdom Beyond books, and the story of the Seven Brothers Champak comes from the *Thakurmar Jhuli* story of shat bhai chompa—seven princes who were turned into champak flowers by their evil stepmothers. Queen Pinki, the rakkhoshi who appears in this series as well as the Kingdom Beyond and Fire Queen series, is modeled after an actual rakkhoshi queen from *Thakurmar Jhuli*.

Thakurmar Jhuli stories are still very popular in West Bengal and Bangladesh, and have inspired translations, films, television cartoons, comic books, and more. Rakkhosh are very popular as well—the demons everyone loves to hate—and appear not just in folk stories but also Hindu mythology. Images of bloodthirsty, long-fanged rakkhosh can be seen everywhere—even on the backs of colorful Indian trucks and auto-rikshaws, as a warning to other drivers not to tailgate or drive too fast!

Tuntuni

The wisecracking bird Tuntuni also appears in the Kiranmala books. Tuntuni is a favorite, and recurrent, character of Bengali children's folktales. Upendrakishore Ray Chowdhury (also known as Upendrakishore Ray) collected a number of these stories starring the clever tailor bird Tuntuni in a 1910 book called *Tuntunir Boi (The Tailor Bird's Book)*.

Astronomy

As with the other books set in the Kingdom Beyond multiverse, there are several references to the multiverse in *The Poison Waves*. These ideas stem from string or multiverse theory, the notion that there may exist—in parallel to one another—many universes, which are simply not aware of the other universes' existences. String/multiverse theory appears in all the Kingdom Beyond books because it feels in keeping with the immigrant experience—the idea that immigrant communities are space explorers and universe-straddlers.

That said, please don't take anything in this book as scientific fact, but rather, be like Kiya and use the story to inspire some more research about astronomy, black holes, and string theory!

Environmental Justice

The Secrets of the Sky series is inspired by the work that so many young people around the world are doing involving climate and environmental justice. Kiya and Kinjal learn in *The Poison Waves* how acid rain can hurt the seas and those creatures living in the water. They also learn, at the end of the story, how changes in the climate can cause destructive floods, mudslides, storms, and more. Ultimately, in the web of nature and life, everything is connected to everything.

The first step toward helping take action to heal our planet is, of course, learning about climate change and the environment. I hope this story inspires some readers to learn more about the science behind these issues—to incorporate both Kinjal's love of story and Kiya's love of science to become champions for our earth and environment! As

Kiya and Kinjal learn, the enemy of change is the Great Blah, or ennui—that feeling of "what can I do anyway?" and "why bother?" Caring is the opposite of this terrible monster of blah-ness; it is the magic, I hope, that will help save our planet and all the people on it.

✦ ACKNOWLEDGMENTS ✦

When the waves of self-doubt or feelings of overwhelm threaten to pull me under, I'm so lucky to have a team that keeps me afloat, and—like the flying pakkhiraj horses in the Secrets of the Sky series—gives my stories wings. Thank you to my agent, Brent Taylor, for believing in me and always lifting me up. Endless thank-yous to my brilliant editor, Abigail McAden. You both make me hopeful about this world that we're creating, one story at a time.

Thank you to Sandara Tang and Elizabeth Parisi for the beauty of this cover and the book's illustrations. Gratitude to Melissa Schirmer, my production editor; Jessica White, my copy editor; and to the rest of my Scholastic family including Ellie Berger, David Levithan, Rachel Feld, Lizette Serrano, Emily Heddleson, Seale Ballenger, and Lia Ferrone! Thank you to the team from Scholastic Book Clubs and the team from Scholastic Book Fairs, for getting this series into the hands of so many readers.

Thank you to all those author friends I've made on this

journey, including my We Need Diverse Books, KidLit Writers of Color, and Desi Writers families. Thank you to my narrative medicine/health humanities colleagues and students at Columbia and around the country. Thank you to my extended family, as well as my wonderful Bengali immigrant community of aunties, uncles, and friends.

To my beloved parents, Sujan and Shamita; my husband, Boris; and my darlings, Kirin, Sunaya, and Khushi—love and magic, magic and love. Because everything is connected to everything. And you are my everythings.